THE COMEDIAN

A Tragedy in Two Acts by

GORDON HINCHEN

ISBN: 979-8-218-40201-3

ISBN 979-8-218-40201-3
50999>

9 798218 402013

1

For Production Inquiries
Wrender Studios
Please visit: www.scriptdoctoratl.com
Or email: wrenderstudiosllc@gmail.com

THIS MEDITATION ON GRIEF AND
ALCOHOLISM IS FOR ALL THOSE UNLUCKY
ENOUGH TO FALL PREY TO THEIR INVITING
ALLURE

TO MY LOVING WIFE
KELSEY
Thank you for always believing in me when no one else would. I could not have done this without you, nor would I want to do it without you. I love you, always.

TO MY PARENTS
Thank you for your love and support throughout my life. Most people will never enjoy the privilege of having two loving and supportive parents, so my gratitude cannot be overstated.

TO MY MANY MENTORS
Thank you, Tom Fulton, for sharing with me your love and expertise in Shakespeare. This was the very spark that ignited me.
Thank you, Bernadette Clemens, for helping me see who I was and what I could become.
Thank you, Mitchell Fields, Bob Ellis, and the late, great Jimmy Green, for helping me develop, not just as an artist, but as a man.
Thank you, Nathan Motta and Chris Bohan for trusting me with my first equity production and being excellent examples of ever-professionals.
And thank you, Malik J. Ali, for always going out of your way to support me and help me grow as an artist and businessman while never asking for anything in return.

And a special thank you to my business partners at Wrender Studios.
Thank you, Jon Heus, for reading and giving notes on every new draft. Your feedback was invaluable and played a major role in shaping the final product. And thank you, Ford Smith, for providing a new perspective on the previous draft and giving me just what I needed to tie everything together, as well as doing all the heavy-lifting in producing the very first staged reading.

And finally, I'd like to thank you, the reader, for supporting my work. If you'd like to support in other ways, please consider leaving a review or contacting me directly at wrenderstudiosllc@gmail.com to obtain the rights to produce my work!

Without further delay, please enjoy my freshman dramatic effort,

THE COMEDIAN

CAST
(9: 5m, 4f)

ROBIN. A retired comedian, 41, m.

ALICE. Robin's now orphaned niece, 16, f.

AUGUST. Alice's boyfriend, 17, m.

ADAM. Alice's father, 40s-50s, m.

EVE. Alice's mother, Robin's sister 40s-50s, f.

SARAH. Robin's ex-wife, 20s, f.

LUIS. Robin's housekeeper, trans, 60s, m.

TONY. Chief of Police, bald, 60s, m.

AURORA. Reporter, 30s-40s, f.

DOUBLING

SARAH/AURORA

ADAM/TONY (optional)

SCENE BREAKDOWN

6

PLACE

PAST: Alice's rundown trailer park home.

PRESENT: Robin's secluded Hollywood mansion.

NOTE: Use lighting to distinguish between the two

spaces.

TIME

Present.

NOTE

A (/) indicates when the next character's dialogue

should begin.

WARNING

Act II, Scene 2.5 can be triggering. It depicts an act

of suicide. Therefore, I grant producers/directors full

authority to cut entirely or edit at their discretion.

Read or stage at your own risk.

THE COMEDIAN

ACT I

Scene 1: Alice in the Golden Afternoon

SETTING: ***Alice's home. A week ago.*** *A rundown, disheveled trailer park living room. There's a couch in the middle of the room, a piano off to the side and a make-shift kitchen in the corner.*

AT RISE: *The LIGHTS are OUT. ALICE - female, 16, wearing hand-me-downs - and AUGUST - male, 17, meek, in tattered rags more than clothes, black coal stained to his jeans and finger nails - are cuddled up on the couch under a cover.*

AUGUST. Charlotte... What do you think of that?

ALICE. The pig? Absolutely not!

AUGUST. Charlotte's the spider. She does everything she can to save her friend, but in the end it's her that needs saving.

ALICE. Dude, way to lighten the mood.

AUGUST. It's not sad, it's inspiring. To live for something other than yourself. To die knowing you've left the world a better place.

ALICE. Well, when you put it like that... it's ok I guess.

AUGUST. Charlotte... what a beautiful name. Not like mine: August. Everything dies in August.

ALICE. No, nature hits the pause button to avoid dying. Winter is harsh so it's better to bunker down in the meantime. And sure, some things will die, but not everything. August is nature choosing life over death.

AUGUST. What about your name?

ALICE. Alice?

AUGUST. Yeah! What's it mean?

ALICE. You know the kids books? *Alice in Wonderland*?

AUGUST. Not really.

ALICE. What kid hasn't read *Alice's Adventures in Wonderland*?

AUGUST. ...No one ever taught me to read. No one ever cared about me... not 'til you came along.

ALICE. So you can't read, but somehow you know *Charlotte's Web*?

AUGUST. Well yeah, it's a movie.

ALICE. So is *Alice in Wonderland*!

AUGUST. Well I never seen it.

ALICE. Sure. Anyway, that's what my dad named me after. I don't know what it means though.

AUGUST. Charlotte... I'm nothin' - I'm no one - but at least I can leave behind somethin' good in this world.

ALICE. I didn't know you cared so much.

AUGUST. I didn't. But everything's changed now.

ALICE. We don't even know if it's a girl yet.

AUGUST. It's a girl. It has to be.

ALICE. And if it isn't?

AUGUST. Then God help us. 'Cause I ain't ready to raise no man. I'm still a boy myself.

ALICE. No you're not. You're a man. And it takes a man to raise a girl too, ya know? I love my mom, but if it weren't for my dad... I don't know where I'd be--

(*The LIGHTS cut ON, revealing ADAM, ALICE's father, standing behind the couch with a PISTOL in AUGUST's mouth. ADAM is as calm and measured as the day is long.*)

ADAM. Bite down... harder. (*AUGUST obliges.*) Now get up. (*AUGUST, not letting go of the pistol in his mouth, stands and tracks backward. ADAM, finger massaging the trigger, remains completely STOIC.*) I'm gonna ask you a few questions. When it's your turn to talk, you're

9

gonna take your mouth off the barrel and give me a clear and concise answer. It will be your inclination to lie or tell a half-truth. Don't. If you're honest with me, this will all be over soon.

ALICE. Dad--

ADAM. Men are talking, sweetheart. Don't interrupt. First thing's first. What's your name, son?

(AUGUST does just as instructed. He unclenches his jaw and severs the connection between his mouth and the pistol.)

AUGUST. (*Sweating.*) August.

ADAM. August, if you had to guess - and you do - whose house do you think this is?

AUGUST. Yours.

ADAM. And as a man, do you think it's appropriate to enter another man's house without asking permission?

AUGUST. No, sir.

ADAM. So we agree. How then would you assess my response, given the circumstances?

AUGUST. Understandable.

ADAM. If you were me, would you do the same?

AUGUST. No.

ADAM. What would you do?

AUGUST. Let the punk go.

ADAM. Is that what you are? A punk?

AUGUST. I'm nothin'. I'm no one.

ADAM. I disagree. You're a man. Just as Alice keenly pointed out. And men aren't nothing. Men take responsibility. Tell me - as a man - if you knew this was my house, why then did you make yourself at home - on *my* couch, with *my* daughter - without asking me a damn thing?

AUGUST. I - I - I don't know. I just-

ADAM. You just, what?

AUGUST. I don't know. I just-

(ADAM points the gun at the floor and - BANG - he fires a round, then points it back at AUGUST.)

ADAM. (*Louder.*) Be honest, son. I'm a grown man. I can

10

take it.

AUGUST. (*Shouting.*) I didn't want you to know I was here!

ADAM. (*Matching AUGUST's volume.*) Go on! Give it to me straight!

AUGUST. I was afraid of what you might think!

ADAM. About what, August?! What were you doing that you were so afraid I might find out about?!

AUGUST. Your daughter! I was doing your daughter!

    (*A silence. ADAM, despite his volume, retains his composure. ALICE and AUGUST are desperately fearful of what comes next. To their reprieve:*)

EVE. (O.S.) What's all that noise?! Is everything ok?!

    (*EVE, ALICE's mom, ENTERS carrying groceries. She steps inside and stops dead. The groceries drop to the floor.*)

EVE. (CONT'D) Adam, baby, put the gun down. (*ADAM doesn't move or lose his composure.*) Talk to me, baby. What's the kid done?

    (*A moment while ADAM considers the query. Severely undercutting the tension, ADAM lowers the gun and breaks out in a fit of sadistic laughter.*)

ADAM. Nothing! (*ADAM embraces AUGUST, kissing his forehead.*) Just caught the kids having a little too much fun. Ain't that right?

AUGUST. Uh - uh - yes, sir.

ADAM. Let me help you with those, Eve, darling. (*ADAM tucks his pistol away and helps EVE with the groceries.*) Boy, y'all are easy to fuck with. You should'a seen your faces... Alice, baby, do your legs not work?

    (*ALICE gets up from the couch and helps put away the groceries.*)

ALICE. Fridge is full, just so you know.

ADAM. I'll make room. (*At the fridge.*) Here, we'll finish off these brews. August, think fast. (*ADAM tosses AUGUST a beer. AUGUST catches it, although clumsily. ADAM pops open his beer then tosses the bottle opener to AUGUST. He opens his beer, though*

not as smooth. It fizzes over as a result of being tossed.)
CHEERS! Don't worry about the mess.

AUGUST. Cheers.

ADAM. To being a man.

> *(ADAM enjoys his beer. He doesn't shotgun it but he's not shy about drinking it either. He squinches. There's something about the taste.)*

EVE. Just as God intended.

ALICE. I don't think he anticipated men being so obnoxious.

EVE. Boys will be boys. (*Approaching AUGUST.*) I'm mom - officially - but you can call me Eve. And you are?

ALICE. Oh my God, I'm sorry mom. This is August. My-

AUGUST. Friend.

ADAM. Close friend. Real close.

EVE. Don't mind him. He's a teddy bear. But never in front of an audience.

ADAM. What are you, a glorified koozie? Drink.

ALICE. A warm beer is a sin in this house.

> *(AUGUST drinks his beer.)*

AUGUST. I should get going.

EVE. It was nice meeting you. You're welcome any time.

AUGUST. Bye Alice.

ADAM. (*Imitating ALICE.*) Bye August. Call me. (*Dropping the imitation.*) Seriously. Call next time.

ALICE. Bye August.

AUGUST. Bye.

ALICE. Bye.

> *(AUGUST grabs his backpack sitting next to the couch and swiftly EXITS. EVE sharply drops her pleasant demeanor and HITS ADAM.)*

EVE. You maniac! Are you fucking crazy? What the hell was that about?

ADAM. Why don't you ask innocent Miss Alice.

ALICE. So we were on the couch together. Big deal.

ADAM. Snuggled up under a cover. In the dark.

EVE. I don't care what she did. You pulled a gun on a

terrified kid. Alice, are you ok?

ALICE. I'm fine mom. Dad just overreacted. I think August will be ok, too. Please, let's not fight.

ADAM. Fucking pussy left his beer.

(ADAM chugs the left-behind beer, squinching again from the taste.)

EVE. (*Breaking down.*) I'm so sick of this. I don't know how much more I can take.

ADAM. Are you really that upset? The kid had it coming.

EVE. It's been a long day. I'm taking a nap. When I wake up, I want you gone... Oh, Allie, I'm so sorry. How'd the dress do?

ALICE. (*Embarrassed.*) Mom! (*Privately.*) It did the trick.

(EVE EXITS. ADAM brushes off EVE's excitement as if it were routine. He grabs a warm bottle of cheap whiskey from the cabinet and sips easy.)

ADAM. Now that's more like it. Alice, baby, do me a favor and let that lying sack o'shit Charlie know he's got two days to give me my money back he swindled for this garbage he cooked up in that out-house he calls a brewery. Scratch that, I'mma tell him myself. My fist being the messenger.

ALICE. I thought you liked Charlie's home brews. His stouts are your go-to's.

ADAM. (*Joining ALICE on the couch.*) I never liked his piss-beer. I just liked that he couldn't distill for shit. He'd say 8% but they'd be 20%, easy.

ALICE. He spiked yours on purpose 'cause he knew you'd be back for more so long as he did.

ADAM. Well this time he didn't and I want my money back.

ALICE. Mom picked those up. Maybe he thought they were for her.

ADAM. God love that woman. I'm a rotten piece of shit, you know. I'd be nothing without your mother.

ALICE. Do you really love her?

ADAM. Of course, baby. I love her like nobody's business. I know a lot of craziness happens between her

13

and I, but you don't ever have to question that.

ALICE. Then why do you do everything you can to fuck things up?

ADAM. Because, baby, I'm a mess. I got demons in my head. Real dark shit. I see snakes in the grass everywhere I go. It keeps me paranoid. Keeps me acting a fool. But your mom sets me straight as I grow crooked. I need her. More than you need air... Your uncle - that's your mom's brother - he's got demons too. You seen the news?

ALICE. No.

ADAM. Man's a trainwreck - though I'm not one to speak. Called 911 to report a death at his residence. Cops showed up to find him passed out on the floor. Tried to hang himself but the rope gave way.

ALICE. God must have other plans for him.

ADAM. Your mother's not here right now: you don't have to play religious.

ALICE. I'm not playing. It's just a phrase.

ADAM. Well, I hope someone has plans for him. Being family and all, I called to check up. Apparently he's at a facility to help "rehabilitate" him. You know, suicidal thoughts, depression, alcohol, etc.

ALICE. Alcohol is cool though, right?

ADAM. It can make sane men do terrible things. Your uncle was an amazing man before...

ALICE. The alcohol?

ADAM. Sure. Funniest man I ever met.

ALICE. I know. You've shown me the clips.

ADAM. That's just his stand-up. Which - ok, yeah - that's what made him famous, but in person he was a different beast entirely. Sucks this snowflake society canceled him for "hate speech." Whatever the Hell that is. (*Nostalgia gets the better of him.*) Every line was a joke funnier than the last. Every time he opened his mouth. Every single time. It was like nothing I'd ever seen. He was a force of nature. And he did it all without ever insulting anyone individually. He only made fun of himself and people in general, but never someone else by name. Nowadays, comics have no class. They'll name your grandmother if it'll give them clicks. Clout chasers, all of them.

ALICE. I thought you hated him. Why the nostalgia? (*ADAM offers ALICE a sip.*) No thanks.

ADAM. Don't tell me you're pissed too?

ALICE. No. Just not in the mood.

ADAM. Guess they really do sync up. Like mother like daughter.

> (*ADAM takes a generous gulp. It bites hard, but he doesn't show it.*)

ALICE. (*Uncomfortable.*) Dad...

ADAM. Right, sorry... No, it's just... Robin's a real son-of-a-bitch. I love and I hate him. I hate him - not for all the reasons everyone else does, that's just haters being haters - but for shit he's done to us personally. That man... he's got a lot to answer for. Robin's a stain on this Earth. For reasons I can't get into. But then again, so am I. Only good thing I ever did was raise you to be a beautiful young woman. And, in a way, he gave us you. And so I love him for that. (*ADAM puts his hand on ALICE's lap. ALICE, uncomfortable, moves his hand to the couch cushion.*) Was he your boyfriend?

ALICE. NO! Dad-- EW! No. He's just like some awkward kid I felt bad for. You saw him just now, but you should'a seen him before. He was such a nerd. Now look at him. I made him cool... cool adjacent.

ADAM. Did you...?

ALICE. Oh God no! Dad, for real?

ADAM. He seems to think you did.

ALICE. Well yeah like once, but like... that was it.

ADAM. Listen to me, no man's ever gonna love you like I do.

ALICE. I know that.

ADAM. I mean it. (*Beat. ADAM takes another generous gulp.*) I liked him.

ALICE. No you didn't.

15

ADAM. You brought him over just to make me jealous.

(Once again, ADAM puts his hand on ALICE's lap. She endures the advance a moment longer than last before repositioning his hand to a cushion. ADAM's grip on the cushion intensifies as if he were in need of an outlet for his aggression. While clutching the furniture, he discovers something wedged between the cushions: A PREGNANCY TEST. A SHOCK comes over ALICE. ADAM is MORTIFIED.)

ALICE. Dad, I can explain--

ADAM. It's positive.

ALICE. Please don't be upset--

ADAM. She's pregnant.

ALICE. I was only hiding it because--

ADAM. That BITCH!

(ADAM jumps up, enraged, unholstering his pistol. ALICE desperately attempts to calm him down.)

ALICE. WAIT! Dad, STOP!

ADAM. That son-of-a-bitch! She cheated on me. It's been almost a year since we've been intimate!

ALICE. Dad, NO!

(ADAM EXITS to the bedroom where EVE is trying to sleep. ALICE tries a different tactic: she races to the landline and calls 911.)

[NOTE: The following off stage (O.S.) dialogue can be muffled and indeterminable so long as it is chaotic, loud, and messy.]

ADAM. (O.S.) You fucking whore!

EVE. (O.S.) *(Waking.)* Wha-what?

ADAM. (O.S.) Who was it? Was it Charlie? That piss-beer-brewing, conniving prick!

EVE. (O.S.) Baby, put the GUN DOWN.

[NOTE: This O.S. dialogue continues improvised and indistinguishable during the following phone call.]

16

ALICE. (*On the phone*.) Send help! Please!... Send whoever! Just - just please - just send someone!... 87 Elm Drive. Hurry! It's my dad, he's -- yeah that house. That's the one! Exactly, exactly! The same as before!

EVE. (O.S.) Baby... I'm telling the truth. You have to believe me. I don't know what that is. I only cheated that one time... I thought we were past this...

ADAM. (O.S.) Evidently, not.

EVE. (O.S.) Baby--

(GUN FIRE drowns the noise, depriving us of knowing EVE's last words. ALICE drops the phone without hanging up and sprints O.S. to her mother's side. ADAM ENTERS, bloodied, with his gun in one hand and whiskey in the other, emotionless. After some time, ALICE ENTERS, blood-soaked.)

ALICE. YOU BASTARD! You killed her! You took her from me!... It wasn't even hers. It was mine. I'm the one who's pregnant.

(BEAT.)

ADAM. Is it mine?

(ALICE is too distraught to respond. Red and blue flashing lights puncture the windows and paint the walls. A moment passes. ADAM is resolute. He downs the last of the whiskey and puts the gun to his temple... BANG. Simultaneously, before the carnage can be witnessed:)

LIGHTS OUT.

17

ACT I

Scene 2: After All These Years

SETTING: ***Robin's home***. *Wealthy suburban living room with an opening to the kitchen and a terrific view of the lush green overgrowth through the sliding glass doors. Extremely spacious. The old chandelier provides an aged accent to the modern aesthetic of the house. A tattered rope hangs from an overhead beam. Despite the WARM tones, the lighting is COOL.*

AT RISE: *The sound of heavy downpour DROWNS the silence. A FLASH of light, followed by THUNDER. The dreadful weather persists throughout the scene.*

The front double doors BURST open, as if kicked. ENTER SARAH, female, 24, WILD hair, WILD eyes, jean short-shorts, tattoos, and up to absolutely no good. She plants herself dead center in the room, taking in the space. The moment achieves a nefarious flare with the BOOM of thunder and dramatic flashes of lightning, taking SARAH in and out of SILHOUETTE. SARAH proceeds to make herself at home. She prepares a glass of scotch - Johnnie Walker Blue, double, straight up. She makes her way to the couch, sits down, and throws her feet up. SARAH grabs the remote from its clearly designated home and turns on the TV. The tremendous HUM of the home theatre's base proves both therapeutic and somewhat erotic to SARAH. She SWOONS and COOS.

As the hum subsides, distant voices SHOCK SARAH into a state of emergency. She cuts off the TV and carelessly tosses the remote on the couch. SARAH struggles to gulp down her scotch. Running out of time, she leaves the non-empty tumbler on the bar. Two figures appear behind the sliding glass doors, DRENCHED and weary. SARAH expeditiously DIVES under the couch. Miraculously, she is just small enough to fit, albeit barely.

ENTER ALICE, ripped jeans, make-up running, brandishing a tattered and now SOAKED suitcase over her head. Struggling to BREATHE, she ransacks her suitcase. No time to spare: as soon as she finds her inhaler, she squeezes the trigger, draws in deep, and holds her breath. She counts to ten, then exhales.

ENTER ROBIN, male, 41, thick beard and dirty hair, designer (traditional black & white) tux, price tag still attached to his jacket, physically disheveled, practically DELIGHTED by the state of affairs.

ROBIN. Well. That was fun.
    (ALICE breaks out in a fit of LAUGHTER, although it is unclear why. ROBIN flicks ON the house LIGHTS. Too bright, he dims them.)
ALICE. I'll say. Next time, don't forget your keys.
ROBIN. Never needed them before.
    (The storm RIPS the sliding glass doors OPEN and heavy wind and rain POUR in. ALICE rushes to close the doors, ROBIN follows sluggishly behind. Once closed, ALICE locks the doors. Beat.)
ROBIN. Sorry about the mess. I've... been away.
ALICE. We must be from different worlds.
ROBIN. I know it's nothing fancy, but-
ALICE. Are you kidding me? This place is incredible. Perfect for the next two days.
ROBIN. Stay. Please. I could use the company.
ALICE. Two days. And then I'm gone. *(ALICE turns her*

luggage upside down, DUMPING it all to the floor.)

ROBIN. Sorry about your jeans.

ALICE. Nah, they're lowkey dope now.

ROBIN. The stains add character.

ALICE. Sure. We'll go with that.

ROBIN. I'll give you some money to go shopping later.

ALICE. Dude, what? Just clean them.

ROBIN. Right. The Puerto Rican chick who handles that sorta stuff - Luisa or something - comes in at... well I don't really know, but she's-

ALICE. Perfect. We'll just wait for the professional.

ROBIN. Or maybe I could do it.

ALICE. They're not designer clothes. Just toss them in the wash.

ROBIN. You got it.

ALICE. Think you can handle that?

ROBIN. I'm no Luisa, but I'll give it the ol' college try.

ALICE. Wait! Let me change first so you can wash these clothes too.

ROBIN. It's your world, I'm just livin' in it.

(ALICE holds up a dress in a plastic cover.)

ALICE. I hate to wear this, but I don't have much of a choice.

ROBIN. *(Recognizing it.)* That's a beautiful dress.

ALICE. Exactly. Mom gave it to me. For my birthday. She caught me trying it on one day for a date. It's her favorite. Says it brings good luck.

ROBIN. Wasn't always hers.

ALICE. Really? Whose was it?

ROBIN. Shower's back there. Help yourself-- oh wait, let me just grab somethin' real quick.

(ROBIN swiftly EXITS to the bathroom and RETURNS just as fast with a bottle of red wine.)

ALICE. Red wine?

ROBIN. Not just any red wine. VINTAGE 1959 RED BORDEAUX. *Very* hard to find.

(ROBIN tucks the bottle away for later.)

ALICE. You keep that shit in your bathroom?

ROBIN. Not usually. It was a special occasion.

ALICE. In your bathroom?

ROBIN. It was a *very* special occasion.

ALICE. Got it. (*ALICE EXITS to the powder room.*)

ROBIN. First floor on your left... DOOR! First door.

(*ROBIN tosses ALICE's clothes into the washer. A dense FLOP is heard as ALICE throws her wet clothes into the living room. Collecting them, ROBIN adds them to the washer. He stares at it for a moment, then with a 'fuck it' attitude turns the dials to whatever settings and starts the washer. ROBIN takes his phone out of his pocket, types something, then shoves it back in. ALICE ENTERS wearing the dress. ROBIN does not immediately notice.*)

ROBIN. (*Too proudly.*) I took care of it.

ALICE. (*Appropriately unimpressed.*) Cool.

ROBIN. Your stuff. It's washing as we speak. (*Finally noticing the dress.*) Wow. Wow, that's- (*A low rumble from the storm cuts him off.*)

ALICE. Too much?

ROBIN. No. It's perfect. You look... just like her.

ALICE. Is that alright?

ROBIN. It's more than alright.

(*ALICE turns her back to ROBIN. The zipper to her dress is down, revealing her bare back.*)

ALICE. Do you mind?

(*ROBIN obliges, zipping up her dress, his skin touching hers.*)

ROBIN. One could almost say she lives.

ALICE. Don't. You weren't there. You didn't see what I saw. I tried to stop him, but he had this look in his eyes. No anger, no pain. Just an emptiness... If there's one thing you can trust me on, it's that she's no longer of this Earth. And I'm all that's left to suggest she ever was.

(*Lighting STRIKES. The chandelier CHIMES, sweetly. ROBIN walks over to the living room*) *dresser and pulls out a smooth black casing. From it, he withdrawals a diamond NECKLACE.)*

ROBIN. This was my late wife's. A family heirloom. It was their tradition to hand it down to the eldest daughter. When she passed, I kept expecting her family to come looking for it. But they never came. Maybe they just wanted to move on. Sometimes it feels like I'm the only one who hasn't.

ALICE. *(Pretending to be made of stone.)* Cool story bro.

ROBIN. *(Not paying her adolescence any mind.)* I know what it's like being all that's left of someone. You never have to feel alone here.

ALICE. *(Dropping the act.)* It's beautiful.

ROBIN. Take it. It's yours.

ALICE. Shut up. You better not be teasing me, dude.

ROBIN. For 16 years it's been collecting dust. Such a shame to keep this jewel hidden from the world. I know she'd want you to have it.

(ROBIN brushes back ALICE's hair as he hangs the necklace about her neck, their faces nearly touching. As he stands back, she lets out a high-pitched SHRIEK.)

ALICE. Mom never lets me wear jewelry. Says it'll drive the boys crazy. I never understood that. Who cares what it'll do to the boys? I'm only interested in men. *(ROBIN stands stunned, DUMBFOUNDED.)* I promise, I'll give it back before I go. In case her family ever comes looking for it.

ROBIN. Don't you dare. Their tradition is yours to keep now. If you're ever lucky enough to have a daughter of your own. *(BEAT. ALICE drags her palm across her stomach. ROBIN is quick to misinterpret as always.)* You hungry?

ALICE. Uncle Robin-

ROBIN. Robin. Just Robin. Uncle was my father's name.

ALICE. Thank you.

ROBIN. Any time, kid. Now tell me what I did.

ALICE. Made me feel normal again. I've spent the entire

last week being spoken to like a lost puppy.

ROBIN. Welcome to Holly-jackass-wood! Most adults here in La La Land have spent their entire lives sheltered from the rest of the world. They've never experienced any real pain. They see people like us and think their pity will magically mend our brokenness. Because they themselves thrive off others' pity. Their hippie-dippie parents taught them that words were bullets and silence was violence. They champion tolerance above all else, but can't tolerant an opposing point of view. I was the last of a dying breed. A comedian who told jokes that were actually funny. But they sent us the way of the dodo. Now all that's left are late-night puppets with activists for writers. How's that for pity?

ALICE. Been stewing over that one for a while, huh?

ROBIN. I was "The" comedian. Now that title is enjoyed by all manner of humor-less succubi. The profession is dead. They killed it. Comedians are no more. I don't know what I am now. Nothing, I suppose... no one.

(Beat.)

ALICE. Dad doesn't seem to think so. He thinks you've still got it.

ROBIN. Has your asthma always been that bad?

ALICE. Not 'til recently.

ROBIN. I had asthma too, ya know.

ALICE. Had?

ROBIN. When I was your age. But I grew out of it. Most people do.

ALICE. The sooner the better. I had to give up soccer last year. It wasn't a big deal in middle school, but at freshmen tryouts I just couldn't keep up anymore.

ROBIN. Must've inherited it.

ALICE. Not that I can tell.

ROBIN. Right.

ALICE. I'm glad you figured it out all by yourself.

ROBIN. Me too.

(ROBIN nods his head confidently in agreement but

clearly has no idea to what ALICE is referring.)

ALICE. The washer.

ROBIN. Yes! The washer. Luisa or whatever - she's not the hottest chick in the room - not even if the room were a chicken coop - but when it comes to cleaning my dirty laundry, her talents are unrivaled. There's no question. However, yes, I figured it out.

ALICE. And you started it already?

ROBIN. All taken care of.

ALICE. How come you didn't toss in your own wet clothes?

ROBIN. (*A moment of reflection.*) Hm.

ALICE. You're literally dripping everywhere. If I slip and fall, I'm gonna kill you.

ROBIN. Then you'll really be all alone.

ALICE. On second thought, why wait?

(ALICE draws a meat knife from the rack, but before she can swing, ROBIN grabs her from behind. He quickly gains control of her wrist and DISARMS her. They take in the closeness of the moment. Breaking apart, ROBIN lets out an exhaustive HUFF. Beat. ROBIN and ALICE KEEL over in uncontrollable laughter.)

ALICE. (CONT'D) You can stop the washer and add your clothes.

ROBIN. Can a man stop a train that's already left the station?

ALICE. I don't know, dude.

ROBIN. I don't know either - DUDE - and maybe that's the point. (*ALICE giggles at ROBIN's silliness.*) C'mon. I'll show you where you'll be sleeping from now on. A master bedroom fit for a queen.

ALICE. Dude, I told you. Two days. That's it.

ROBIN. (*Mocking.*) Dude. Dude. DUDE. DUUUDE. (*Letting that go.*) I'm just tryna show you your room.

ALICE. Not now. I'm fucking starving, dude.../ And I hardly think I'm deserving of the royal treatment.

ROBIN. Ah ha! I knew it! Well dude, there's plenty of

food in the-- oh. I guess you found it.

ALICE. Yeah most people keep their food in the fridge and shit, so. (*ALICE opens the fridge. It's FULL of BEER, surprisingly organized.*) HOLY-- Uncle Robin! There's nothing but beer in here.

ROBIN. No need to twist my arm, dude. Just take one. You've earned it-- I mean... you know what I mean.

ALICE. I want food, not-- wait, for real?

ROBIN. Yeah. Just one though... Fuck it, toss me one too.

ALICE. I'm 16.

ROBIN. Better late than never. (*ALICE nervously obliges, tossing ROBIN a beer and taking one for herself.*) Cheers.

ALICE. Cheers. To not giving two fucks.

ROBIN. I'll drink to that.

(*ROBIN CHUGS his beer as if to drown a painful memory, SPILLING half of it on himself. ALICE cautiously takes a sip and nearly GAGS. Nevertheless, she persists.*)

ALICE. You shouldn't encourage me to do stuff like this. What if someone finds out? We could get in serious trouble. You more than me.

(*SARAH curiously peaks her head out from under the couch. As ROBIN draws near, she tucks away again.*)

ROBIN. Simmer down, Principal Buzzkill. Life ain't just about livin'. It's about dyin' your way. *And I got a deal with the devil.*

ALICE. Seriously though. I'm fucked up as it is and I don't want to end up like you.

ROBIN. Rich and famous.

ALICE. Washed up and irrelevant.

ROBIN. Yeah I think you've had enough.

(*ROBIN SNATCHES the half-full beer from ALICE and returns it to the fridge.*)

ALICE. Real nice... Isn't the master your room?

ROBIN. Luisa or whatever usually stocks the bottom drawer with sandwiches. Help yourself.

ALICE. Way ahead of you.

(ALICE dives into the bottom drawer of the fridge.)

ROBIN. Every room is my room. And I live alone. But you don't have a home to go back to and that ain't changin' any time soon. So I figure I ought to get used to sharing. Take the master. I want you to have it... besides, I usually pass out on the steps anyway.

ALICE. I appreciate you giving me a place to stay for the weekend, but I don't need your handouts. I can take care of myself.

ROBIN. Don't make me laugh. You're a broke 16-year-old and I have a mansion. I'm not trying to adopt you, just help you out.

ALICE. You're not listening. I don't need your help.

(By now, ALICE has her sandwich on a plate and she's modifying it to her liking. Combining sandwiches and smothering it all in mustard. She's not taking the proper precautions to preserve the perfect condition of her dress.)

ROBIN. Without me, you'll be pregnant and married to a 30-somethin' stoner with face tattoos and no dreams or aspirations.

(Beat. ALICE takes ROBIN's premonitions deeply, personally. She massages her stomach again. This time with both wonder and worry.)

ALICE. So what if I were? Would that really be so bad? Not everyone needs the love of a million strangers to be happy. Honestly, what good has it done you?

ROBIN. You may not *need* my help, but it could do you a whole lotta good.

ALICE. I'm emancipated. So it's really not up to you.

ROBIN. I finally have you back in my life. It'd kill me to lose you again.

ALICE. Don't make *me* laugh. You've never shown any interest in my life.

ROBIN. If you only knew the half of it.

ALICE. I know enough. You got famous at a young age - my age - and it got the better of you. Not your fault. It happens to a lot of young socialites who started from the slums. You had the world at your fingertips. Everybody loved you. Everybody wanted to be you. And for a while, you were the happiest you've ever been. Mom always says, "I never seen him so happy." But good things never last. Eventually, it drove you mad and you ended up in a mental hospital. They wouldn't let you near me until you were... *you* again. But by then, you wanted nothing to do with me. So let's not pretend like anything has changed. I'm not a kid anymore, Uncle. I haven't been for some time now. You'd know that if you ever bothered to call. All it would've taken was a call.

> *(Thunder BOOMS once more, though we need no reminder of the mood. Beat.)*

ROBIN. Was that your first drink?

ALICE. My dad says you're an alcoholic.

ROBIN. Every man's entitled to their own opinion. And no man loved to tell me theirs more than him. *(To himself.)* Even six feet deep, that unholy son-of-a-bitch still gets the last word.

ALICE. What about women?

ROBIN. What about them?

ALICE. Aren't women entitled to their own opinions?

ROBIN. Sure. I just wish they wouldn't share them so fuckin' often. *(Sweetly.)* You being the exception.

ALICE. Mom says all men are pigs.

ROBIN. And by implication, what does that make women? Mud... I can do this all day.

ALICE. Knock yourself out.

ROBIN. For the love of God, don't eat like that!

ALICE. Like what?

ROBIN. An alien that's never been around humans before.

ALICE. Says the recluse who hasn't been seen in public for more than six months, now rocking a beard that could make Zeus blush.

ROBIN. You don't like the beard?

ALICE. Look dude, I'm hungry. And I don't care what I

look like. (*Beat*.) No. That was not my first drink.

ROBIN. Really? He said that?

ALICE. Not in so many words. Dad lets me drink.

ROBIN. Exactly how many words?

ALICE. He says you have a drinking problem.

ROBIN. And you have a counting problem.

ALICE. He lets me drink with him when he comes home late from work and mom is asleep.

ROBIN. And he said *I* have a drinking problem?

> *(ALICE begins to CRY, but successfully holds back the tears. The heavy rain proves oddly soothing, like a mother's LULLABY. ALICE clutches her dress. It comforts her.)*

ALICE. I miss those nights. I've never seen dad smile so much.

ROBIN. I'm sure he was just happy to spend time with you... *Drinking*, I might add!

ALICE. That's what mom says! She says that's why she lets him think she doesn't know.

> *(ALICE ATTACKS her sandwich.)*

ROBIN. Could you please not chew with your mouth open?

ALICE. I mean, fuck, I'll try, Uncle.

ROBIN. And stop talking and eating at the same time. And stop cursing so damn much. And stop calling me Uncle! See, you wouldn't last a week without me in the real world. No one could stand to be around you for more than five minutes with you acting like this.

ALICE. Bro, you need to chill. I haven't been here half an hour and you're already trying to micromanage me. And funny you of all people should criticize me about integrating with society. Ever since being booed off stage, you haven't had the balls to-

> *(A thunderous BOOM cuts ALICE off, as much as the sudden shift in ROBIN's POSTURE. ROBIN retrieves the bottle of Red Bordeaux and pours a glass. It proves too slow. Tired of its ineffectiveness, ROBIN treats his liver to the source. The bottle's*

lips to his, he steals a kiss from death, GULPING down what's left. Just what the doctor ordered. It soothes his aching bones, heart, and all.)

ROBIN. (*Refreshed, yet somehow still sarcastic.*) You're right. I do tend to be a bit controlling. At least that's what Sarah always bitched about. That's the good gospel straight from the horse's mouth. And what a horse she was. (*The couch JUMPS. Certainly a result of SARAH's understandable rage, but ROBIN and ALICE cannot even imagine such a thing.*) This storm is the worst I've seen... second worst... You do you. But I'm serious about the cursing. You're 16. You shouldn't be talking like that.

ALICE. Like what? Like you? (*ROBIN responds with a stern look. ALICE, mouth wide-opened.*) Fine. Sorry-- (*Finishes chewing her food, then swallows.*) I mean... sorry. (*A longer moment.*)

ROBIN. You must be a good student.

ALICE. Oh yeah?

ROBIN. Micromanage. That's a big word. I feel like I only just learned that word a year ago and I'm in my fuckin' 40's.

ALICE. Language!

ROBIN. Touché. Cursing is back on the table and I am a failure as a father figure.

ALICE. It was just an AP word from last semester.

ROBIN. So you are in the advanced classes!

ALICE. Sure.

ROBIN. "Sure." Don't be bashful with me, young lady.

ALICE. Why, because you're like the most famous comedian of all time?

ROBIN. No. I just meant-- look, there's no ego police here. You're allowed to brag and be proud.

ALICE. Fine, dude. I'm *really* smart. People think I'm dumb because I'm quiet in school, but I just like to shut up and observe... and I'm surprisingly strong. I can squat more than some of the boys. OH, and I have a great ass!

THE COMEDIAN

ROBIN. What!?

ALICE. My ass. Guys love my ass.

ROBIN. STOP! Stop talking about your ass, please.

ALICE. Dude, calm down. You insisted I brag about myself so what'd you expect? All that my girlfriends and I talk about are boys, butts, and boobs.

(ALICE delights at how effectively she's making ROBIN cringe. She finishes eating and proceeds to wash her dishes. ROBIN gut LAUGHS, appreciating ALICE's glee at his pain. He approaches the bar and finds the whiskey neat left by SARAH. Not terribly alarmed, he throws it back real quick and prepares a Johnnie Walker Blue in the same tumbler. First he adds an ice sphere, then the scotch. He pours a triple, even as the glass overflows. Unconcerned with the mess, he makes his way to the couch and PLOPS down, facing the TV. Eventually, ALICE joins him. The couch is bumpier than usual. They'll have to get used to it.)

ALICE. (CONT'D) Better watch out. You're not the only comedian still lurking in the shadows, evading extinction. We're making a comeback. Just you watch!

ROBIN. You tease just like her.

(Beat. ROBIN, without looking, reaches for the remote in its usual location. It is not there. Perplexed, he DARTS his head all around searching for it. He spies it on the other side of the couch, beyond ALICE even. ROBIN curiously studies the positioning of the remote.)

ALICE. So, what's it like being uber-famous and whatnot?

ROBIN. I don't know. I'm not *that* famous. (*ROBIN reaches over ALICE's lap to retrieve the remote.*)

ALICE. You're not that *relevant*. But you *are* that famous.

ROBIN. She strikes again.

ALICE. You're trying to tell me you're not dripping in hoes or whatever like every rap song ever would suggest?

ROBIN. Depends on what you mean by "dripping."

30

ALICE. Ew. Robin! (*ALICE WALLOPS ROBIN with a pillow.*)

ROBIN. Five points, Slytherin.

ALICE. Come on. I know you think the world has forgotten about you, but true legends never die. I mean, you were nearly GOAT'ed for that bit about getting consent from a chick with Tourette's. How'd it go again? (*Impersonates ROBIN.*) "Eat my ass!"

ROBIN. (*Impossibly giddy.*) Yeah, yeah!! (*Impersonates himself.*) "You sure? In the middle of this Olive Garden?"

ALICE. "Talk about a tossed salad!" (*Their laughter is UPROARIOUS. Positively infectious, even. Eventually, their laughter dies out. Maybe they riff some more before it does. Afterward, ALICE catches her breath and picks herself up off the floor.*) How long were you guys married?

ROBIN. Excuse me?

ALICE. You and horse face.

> (*ALICE, frustrated that ROBIN clearly has no intention of ever using the remote, takes it from him and turns on the TV.*)

ROBIN. Ugh, don't remind me. (*The TV HUMS itself awake, just as before.*)

ALICE. Holy-- that sound is straight fire, dude.

ROBIN. Don't joke me, dude.

ALICE. I never joke about home theatres.

ROBIN. Thank you! I swear, no one ever appreciates Cleopatra.

ALICE. You named your TV!

ROBIN. Au contraire, Cleopatra is so much more than a TV. She's the whole shebang. Beautiful yet smart. Tender yet imposing. LED, 8K, smart-screen, touch - you name it, she's got it. And her sub-woof purrs so sweet you'll swoon.

ALICE. (*Sudden shift in tone.*) Do you love her?

ROBIN. (*Sensing the shift in ALICE's tone.*) Always.

ALICE. Then why do you talk about her like she's a fat,

ugly broad?

ROBIN. (*Realizing he read the room incorrectly.*) Oh, Sarah? I thought you were talkin' about-- No, I hate Sarah. Sarah is a donkey with a horse's face.

> (*SARAH HEAVES in rage, but it is drowned out by the sudden and coincidental BOOM of thunder. Already done with his drink, ROBIN returns to the bar.*)

ALICE. A mule?

ROBIN. I'd love one, but I'm nursing a *Johnnie Walker Blue* and it'd be a sin to chase it with something sweet.

ALICE. No, Sarah. The donkey with a horse's face.

> (*Refueling, ROBIN once again over pours, worsening the state of the bar. Surely, it is a sticky mess.*)

ROBIN. Absolutely. She's crazy. And I don't mean how guys always say a woman's crazy when they break up. Every guy says that. No, I mean Sarah is INSANE. Wouldn't be surprised if she were hiding under the couch right now.

> (*TERRIFIED, ROBIN throws his gaze to the couch. SARAH becomes perfectly still, not even breathing. Beat.*)

ALICE. If you couldn't stand her, then why did you marry her?

ROBIN. You got a favorite show?

ALICE. Sorta. *Game of Thrones*.

ROBIN. Why "sorta?" Either you like it or you don't, right?

ALICE. Right... it's just, mom doesn't let me watch it. But it's the only thing dad and I both like so he lets me watch it when mom is out with her friends. "Just to spend time with me," as you put it.

ROBIN. (*Unconsciously.*) Drinking, I bet.

ALICE. (*Not hearing ROBIN.*) Mom is always out with her friends. (*An uncomfortable silence.*)

ROBIN. I happen to adore *Game of Thrones*. Bit inappropriate for daddo to let you watch it, but it's not lost on me that I'm being hypocritical here, so what the Hell!

(ROBIN practically jumps at the opportunity to end the conversation. He races to the couch and, without sitting, pries the remote from ALICE's limp hand. Before he can cue it up, ALICE puts another damper on the mood.)

ALICE. It's alright I guess. *(A moment. There's a change in the air.)*

ROBIN. Look, I know it only just happened, but the sooner you accept their fate, the better. You can't keep referring to your parents in the present tense. It'll only make it harder. Trust me, I've made that mistake before. *(The THUNDER weighs in once more. ALICE steals the remote back, turns off the TV and sets the remote down. ROBIN now rejoins ALICE on the couch, taking great care to make sure the remote is returned to its designated home.)* I was 16 when I married her. She was the most beautiful woman I had ever seen.

ALICE. Robin! You were my age when you married Sarah??

ROBIN. Oh Hell no! My dumbass fell under that witch's spell years later on cocaine and *Hennessy*. That's why I don't touch the stuff.

ALICE. COCAINE!?

ROBIN. No, *Hennessy*.

ALICE. No - I mean - you did cocaine?

ROBIN. Just coke, ok. You sound like a narc.

ALICE. I'm saying exactly what you said.

ROBIN. You goin' def, kid? I didn't say cocaine. I said coke. I'm not a narc.

ALICE. You literally did though. You literally said "cocaine."

ROBIN. *(Hushed.)* Would you keep your voice down! Next thing you know, *TMZ* will be doing a story about that time I did blow with McConaughey and DiCaprio in the bathroom at the Oscars.

ALICE. If they do, it'll be because *you* brought it up just

33

now. Not because I said cocaine.

ROBIN. Say it again. I dare you.

ALICE. What do I win if I do?

ROBIN. The opportunity to prove you're not a narc.

> *(ROBIN opens up a jar and pulls out a baggie with white powder, BRANDISHING it to ALICE.)*

ALICE. ROBIN!? Surely, you can't be serious.

ROBIN. (*In his best Leslie Nielsen.*) I am Shirley, and don't call me serious.

ALICE. (*Feeling BRAVE from the alcohol.*) "Eat my Ass!" Let's do this.

ROBIN. Yeah, put your money where your mouth is... or nose.

ALICE. I'm broke. Give me a twenty.

ROBIN. Just another reason you should stay... here's a hundred. Don't snort it all in one place.

> *(ALICE SNORTS the line with a hundred-dollar bill. ROBIN GUMS the left-over powder. ALICE Winces.)*

ALICE. FUCK ME!

ROBIN. HAHA! I'm king of the world!

ALICE. Whatever you say, dude. You're on one right now.

ROBIN. Jealous much?

> *(ROBIN finishes his latest glass of scotch, abandons his tumbler on the bar, and rewards himself with another beer from the fridge.)*

ALICE. In your dreams, old man.

ROBIN. This *is* my dream. You've no idea how happy I am to see you again. *After all these years.*

ALICE. I'd hardly call what we're living in a dream, Robin. A nightmare's more like it.

ROBIN. Nightmares end, ya know. All you need to do is wake up.

ALICE. Not this one. This one will never end.

ROBIN. Oh, for fuck sake. Stop being so lugubrious and cheer up, would ya!

> *(ROBIN tosses ALICE a beer. He fails to realize it's*

*the same beer from earlier that ALICE never
finished. Beer SHOOTS in all directions as the open
can flies through the air and crashes into the wall.
ROBIN and ALICE stare at each other for a
moment.)*

ALICE. Let's try that again.

ROBIN. You gonna catch it this time?

ALICE. That depends. You gonna throw it like a bitch
again?

ROBIN. I just might. (*ROBIN tosses another beer, this
time an unopened can. ALICE makes a clean catch.*)

ALICE. "Lugubrious," huh? Guess I'm not the only AP
student.

ROBIN. "The quality of looking sad or dismal." I'm full
of surprises.

ALICE. You're full of something, alright.

ROBIN. SURPRISE!

*(ROBIN LAUNCHES the empty wine bottle at
ALICE. Unsurprisingly, he misses and it
SHATTERS against the wall. A beat as they try to
determine if that was violent or funny... or both.)*

ALICE. If I drink this and stop being so "lugubrious," will
you stop throwing shit at me?

ROBIN. No promises.

ALICE. Touché. Cheers. (*Funny. Definitely funny.*)

ROBIN. CHEERS! Now, was that so hard? (*ROBIN and
ALICE find their way back to the couch.*)

ALICE. Actually, yes. Being happy is fucking difficult.
Calculus is easier than being happy.

ROBIN. (*Abruptly shifting tone again.*) People seem to
think that we somehow deserve to be happy, just
because. As if we deserve anything in life. Like we're
just owed it from birth. Some kind of divine privilege.
But no. Happiness is life's greatest challenge. You have
to fight to be happy, every day. We ain't owed a damn
thing. Anyone who says different, ain't bein' honest
with themselves. I'm not askin' you to be happy. I'm
just askin' you to grow up and deal with it. Life sucks

and we all just need to learn how to accept that. (*His drunkenness reveals itself.*) When my father brought his black leather belt down upon my mother's bare back with all the fury of Hell and hate poisoning his heart, my mother did not flinch. It's 3am. She's on her knees. With a defiant smile she proclaimed before God and her husband, "You can't hurt me." She was determined to live a life of love. She figured, "I'd rather die happy than live in fear." My father, despite his best efforts, couldn't take her happiness away. She was a fighter. Right up until the day she took her own life. A final act of defiance and middle finger to my father. Me, not so much... I haven't been happy since I was 25. When the only woman I ever loved died in my arms. I fought, and fought, but there was nothing I could do. So I threw in the proverbial towel and haven't fought for anything since. I just grew up and dealt with it. Sometimes I wonder, if mom had learned that lesson, might she still be here? Taking her beatings. Dealing with it. Maybe she wouldn't have felt so compelled to die on her own terms. To be happy. Or maybe she was right all along and I'm the one too weak to do what it takes... It was a stormy night. The worst I had ever seen. My wife died in labor. The birth of our baby girl was too much to handle. For so long, I blamed our daughter. "She took my love away," I'd say. How could I love the thing that killed my wife? That took everything from me? I couldn't. I suffered a nervous breakdown from which I would not recover for more than half a decade. That's about the only part you got right. Three days later, she was adopted by a loving family. I never saw her again... When my wife bled to death on that delivery table, I never got to say goodbye. It happened so fast. Never saw death comin'. But that was the old me. Death couldn't surprise me now if he wanted to. All's I do is drink enough of this here magic potion and voilà, I get to see his ass every night. And I never miss an appointment. (*He drinks. Beat.*) Death never says a word or even acknowledges my presence. Makes me feel kinda dirty. Like I'm spying on him or somethin'. But last night, Death looked me dead in the eye - for the first time ever - and held up three fingers, like so. Cryptic as fuck, but I got the message. I got three more dates with the bastard before he pops the question and drags my drunk ass to the other side, for good. At first I thought, "Why three?" Seemed arbitrary. But then I got the call from my attorney. "Good news and bad news. Good news: you're gonna be a father again. Bad news: you're an only child now. Have a nice day, funny man." And now you're sayin' two more days and you're *Audi 5000*. Well that adds up pretty damn perfectly. So I figure I got tonight and the next two days to wrap up this here shit-show. Maybe see mom again. Tell her I forgive her. That I understand. That is, unless you decide to stay. 'Cause without you, I got nothin' left. All this time, I truly believed the only woman I ever loved died that day. But I was wrong. You're the second. And you have yet to know Death's touch. Please stay. I love you more than you will ever know.

(ALICE STEALS a KISS. SARAH, out of view, snaps a picture with her smartphone. ROBIN instantly RECOILS, horrified. A thunderous BOOM underlines the moment.)

ALICE. You said you loved me.

ROBIN. Not like that. (*Beat.*) I think it's my turn to take a shower.

(Beat. ROBIN EXITS to the shower. ALICE is left alone, humiliated, confused. She takes this opportunity to finish her beer and think things over. Once emptied, she flings the empty can across the room. Thunder RATTLES the chandelier once again. ALICE finds her way to the GRAND PIANO and, although it's not a string instrument, plucks the cords to ROBIN's heart. The LIGHTS come DOWN and a single SPOTLIGHT on ALICE replaces them. Unable to resist, ROBIN emerges trance-like in

nothing but a fresh pair of underwear [designer of course] - still drying his hair with a towel - to hear this angelic crescendo. A second spotlight, albeit softer, illuminates him as well.)

(The spotlights FADE, as the song simmers to an end, and return to the room LIGHTS. ROBIN is locked on ALICE. Starstruck, he cannot take his eyes off of her. Still thinking she is experiencing a private heartbreak, ALICE SOBS aloud. Desperate to take away her pain, ROBIN dashes to her rescue. Her first instinct is to hide her pain, but ALICE is at the end of her rope and is helpless to contain this biblical flood.)

ROBIN. (CONT'D) I know it hurts, but I'm here.

ALICE. It's not that I can't accept their fate. I can. It's that I can't accept why? Why would dad kill my mom? His wife? And then himself? Didn't he know that would hurt me? That I loved them both so much, it might kill me too? He said he loved me. And I believed him. Why would anyone hurt someone they loved the way he hurt me?

ROBIN. I don't know. But I do know that he did love you. He couldn't've been right in the head. The autopsy will give us more answers. He played college ball back in the day. I've seen a few of them lose it before. Nothing anybody could've done. Least of all, you.

ALICE. You're not listening, Robin. I said he loved me. Like, *loved me* loved me.

ROBIN. (*A moment to digest the distinction. Then, EXPLODING.*) That slimy BASTARD!

(ROBIN tries to BREAK any and everything he can get his hands on in an uncontrollable drunken RAGE. ALICE has never been more fearful in her life... save the night her father murdered her mother and then himself.)

ALICE. (*Through her tears.*) It's not what you think, Robin. I'm adopted. Like your baby girl.

(ALICE is SOBBING. ROBIN realizes he's scaring

*her so he CALMS down to ease her suffering.
BEAT.)*

ROBIN. Alice... you *are* my baby girl.

*(ROBIN, afraid of what he might do next,
DISAPPEARS upstairs, taking on a defeated gate.
BEAT. Abruptly, the front double doors SWING
open. LUIS, male, 50s, buff, ENTERS lugging in
several heavy bags. ALICE stares awkwardly at
LUIS for a moment. He stares right back. She wipes
away what tears remain, composing herself.)*

LUIS. You must be Miss Alice.

ALICE. And you are...?

LUIS. Pleased to make your acquaintance. Officially.

ALICE. Right.

LUIS. Is Mr. Summerville home?

ALICE. He just showered. Now he's getting dressed.

LUIS. That's new.

ALICE. Funny. I don't think I've heard my name all day.

LUIS. Understandable. Alice was his late wife's name.
  Before Sarah.

ALICE. Did you know her?

LUIS. That necklace... and that dress... I've not seen them
  in some 16 years. I remember to the day. You must have
  Mr. Summerville feeling nostalgic.

ALICE. The dress is my mother's... was.

LUIS. Indeed it was.

*(LUIS puts his bags down and accosts ALICE. The
beer about the entrance proves obnoxiously
slippery. He does his best to remain professional as
he slips and slides his way over to her. Once in
ALICE's orbit, LUIS patiently wraps his arms
around her as she loosens up and lets him. After a
moment, he takes a small step back and looks her up
and down in stoic bewilderment.)*

LUIS. (CONT'D) (*Teary-eyed.*) It's so lovely to finally see
  you again, Miss Alice.

ALICE. We've met?

LUIS. It's been so long. I'd hardly expect you to

remember.

ALICE. Where are you from? You sound... old fashioned?

LUIS. Heavens no. I gave up drinking years ago.

ALICE. I mean, the way you talk. Are you British?

LUIS. Guilty as charged. Long *lived* the Queen. Though, I should note, I've a pinch of Spanish in me. My mother was quite the adventurer... are we all settled in?

ALICE. Not exactly. My clothes are washing as we speak. Robin took care of everything.

LUIS. He did what! (*In CRISIS mode, LUIS rushes to the washer. Opening it, he is saddened by what he finds*.) I'm so sorry, Miss Alice. It seems you're in the market for a new wardrobe.

ALICE. Guess so.

LUIS. Not to worry. (*Addressing the bags he hauled in*.) Robin requested I pick you up some new outfits on my way over. Perhaps a proper premonition, no?

ALICE. He did?... I didn't think he even noticed.

LUIS. Noticed what, my dear?

ALICE. I wore ripped jeans to the... there was no one there but us, so I guess it didn't matter. But still...

LUIS. It wasn't proper.

ALICE. Right. Anyway, he didn't look my way even once the whole time. So I didn't think he cared... I didn't think anyone would ever care again.

LUIS. Save your pessimism for those witless enough to buy it. You're in wise company here, Miss Alice. I know an optimist when I see one.

ALICE. I do my best not to sulk... but I've never felt pain like this before. It's tying me up in knots.

LUIS. Pain is good. Never shy from it. Embrace it. Lest you fall victim to it... like one such soul I know... Forgive me. Now I'm the one flirting with pessimism.

ALICE. I promise, I won't tell.

LUIS. How lovely. You tease just like her... Come, I'm sure you're eager to lose that dress and snap into something more suitable for lounging. Heaven forbid we tarnish such a treasure.

ALICE. Good point. I don't know what I'd do if anything ever happened to this dress. It's all I've left of her... (*Inspecting the bags*.) *Gucci*, *Armani*, *Louis Vuitton*... I can't accept these.

LUIS. Sure you can. I insist.

ALICE. No, I mean... they're just not me.

(*ROBIN ENTERS in designer lounge wear [i.e. sweatpants, hoodie, no socks]. When his eyes meet LUIS', the world screeches to a halt. The unlikely pair exhibit the rapport of a hundred-year's friendship.*)

ROBIN. LUISA! Not a second too *spoon*.

ALICE. You're Luisa!?

LUIS. The name's Luis, my dear. And what awful things has this fool been saying about me?

ROBIN. Nothin' much. Just that you're the cat's meow. Minus the cat.

LUIS. Letting Miss Alice drink, I see.

ROBIN. Given the circumstances.

LUIS. (*Suddenly serious*.) Your life isn't bad enough, so you have to drag her down with you?

ROBIN. Last week was an accident.

LUIS. (*Glancing up, he spies the rope snapped in two*.) An accident you lived, maybe. (*ROBIN and LUIS EMBRACE, fully and with deep love and empathy. They pull back and take each other in, TEARS in their eyes*.) You look terrible.

ROBIN. I'm not well.

LUIS. Rehabilitation didn't take? Again? There must be another way.

ROBIN. I did real good the first week or so. You'd've been proud of me.

LUIS. You were only in for three days.

ROBIN. Like I said, "or so."

ALICE. (*Genuine*.) Aww. You two are so cute.

LUIS. (*Deeply personal*.) Mr. Summerville and I go way back. He accepted me when no one else would. Even my family wanted nothing to do with me. He *is* my

41

family now.

ROBIN. You've changed though. When we met - some 20 years ago - you had - I never confirmed it, but I assume - a delightful clam betwixt your once dainty legs. Nowadays, I don't know whatcha got goin' on between them tree trunks. Only that I damn sure wouldn't put it anywhere near my mouth.

ALICE. (*Disgusted.*) Robin!

LUIS. Don't be so sure. Curiosity got the cat. Who's to say it won't get you too?

ALICE. (*Concerned.*) Luis!

LUIS. What's that, Miss Alice?

ALICE. You mean, you're not offended?

LUIS. Heavens, no. Words don't hurt, my dear. People do.

ALICE. I get it, I'm no snowflake either, but damn! Those words were beyond mean.

LUIS. I've been beaten and stabbed by those who've never spoken a *mean* word to me. Robin, however, has shown me nothing but kindness. And so, with all due respect Miss Alice, until such time as his actions give me pause to think otherwise, I'll assume his words come from a place of love and respect. I suggest you do the same.

ALICE. (*Under her breath.*) If only it were that easy.

ROBIN. May I have a copy of your keys?

LUIS. But I haven't any, sir.

ROBIN. How the Hell d'you get in, then?

LUIS. The doors were unlocked, sir... the doors are *always* unlocked, sir.

ROBIN. Interesting....

ALICE. Wait, so—oh my God—so we got totally soaked, scaled your ten-foot balcony, and broke into your house for *no* reason?? That's awesome. I'm having a great time.

LUIS. What's this about breaking in? And what's with the mess? My shoes are awfully sticky.

ROBIN. Being a father again is stressful. I'm just taking the edge off.

ALICE. (*Suddenly triggered.*) You are NOT my father. No offense, but my father's more man than you'll ever be.

ROBIN. Maybe two weeks ago. When I was laid out on this hard wood floor. My fat ass snapped that rope up there as it tightened around my neck. My fault. I went to *Wal-Mart* when I should've gone to *Home Depot*. Meanwhile, your daddy - God bless 'm - enjoyed a beautiful dinner with his two favorite girls. Showing them both how *loved* they were. But today? Today, I think he's more *meat* than *man*. And like with my father, we're all the better for it.

LUIS. Robin!

ROBIN. What? /I thought you said words don't hurt.

ALICE. Fuck you! Keep drinking like you do, you'll see him soon enough.

ROBIN. You think he's in Hell, do ya? 'Cause that's where I'm headed. Two days from now.

LUIS. Robin... Two days? Surely you can manage to stay with us a bit longer than that.

ROBIN. I am Shirley, but it's not up to me. /My life is in her hands now.

ALICE. Second time's the charm, huh?

LUIS. How dare you put that on her! She's just a girl.

ALICE. No I'm not! I'm a woman. And I've been through more than most ever will.

LUIS. Apologies, Miss Alice, if I've offended. But I'm not your enemy. Quite the contrary.

(Set off by the abrupt rise in blood pressure, ALICE begins to WHEEZE. She finds her inhaler and does exactly like before, inhaling for ten seconds then exhaling. Beat.)

ALICE. I think I'd like to see my room now.

ROBIN. Of course. Follow me.

LUIS. You've done enough. *(Offering his forearm.)* Miss Alice?

ALICE. *(Accepting.)* Luis.

LUIS. Right this way... You got his lungs, I see. Let's pray that's all you got from him.

(ALICE and LUIS EXIT upstairs with the bags of

new clothes. A moment.)

ROBIN. Wait. I'm giving her the master. First floor on your left... DOOR! First door.

(ROBIN EXITS, following them upstairs. Beat. Beat. From underneath the sofa EMERGES SARAH with an all-too sinister grin. Holding her phone out in front of her, she presses a button and a recording begins to play.)

ROBIN. (V.O.) (*From recording.*) *"All this time, I truly believed the only woman I ever loved died that day. But I was wrong. You're the second. And you have yet to know Death's touch. Please stay. I love you more than you will ever know."*

(A KISSING sound can be heard from the recording, followed by a thunderous BOOM.)

ALICE. (V.O.) (*Recording continues.*) *"You said you loved me."*

ROBIN. (V.O.) *"Not like that."*

(SARAH STOPS the recording. Delighted - almost ditsy - she SKIPS toward the front double doors. Not paying attention, she SLIPS in the beer puddle, falling backward in true comic fashion. The back of her head SMACKS the hardwood floor with a heart-stopping BANG. Glass shards SKEWER her shallow skin.)

ROBIN. (O.S.) What the Hell was that??

(ROBIN RETURNS to find SARAH bleeding out. SARAH EXPIRES, permanently.)

ROBIN. (CONT'D) Hell, indeed. But I still got two days. The devil is in the details.

(Just as soon as ROBIN begins to make his way back upstairs, he gets WOOZY and passes out. Lights FADE to BLUE as the thunder finally subsides and sunlight peaks through the glass doors.)

LIGHTS OUT.

ACT I

Scene 3: Alice in Wonderland

SETTING: *Alice's home. Six weeks ago.*

AT RISE: *ALICE is at the piano, trying out a tune. She's wearing her mother's dress - the same as in the previous scene. Her hair is down. Make-up is laid on a bit thick. Eye-liner, eye-shadow, blush, lip stick, and nail polish. ALICE starts and stops. Eventually, she lands on something she quite likes. She hums along until... A RING at the door.*

ALICE. COMING! (*ALICE goes to answer the door but stops to freshen up. She sprays perfume before her and walks through it. Another RING.*) JUST A SEC!
   (*For good measure, ALICE lifts her dress and sprays a sprits between her legs. The doorbell rings incessantly. RING, RING, RING, RING! ALICE answers the door. Standing on the other side is AUGUST. He's wearing jeans and a stripped polo as well as a rugged backpack.*)
ALICE. (CONT'D) DUDE!
AUGUST. Um, hey...
ALICE. Hey.
AUGUST. Hi.
ALICE. Dude. (*ALICE walks away from the door and heads to the fridge. She stops to look back.*) You comin'?
AUGUST. Sorry. Yes.
   (*AUGUST timidly ENTERS. He stands in the middle of the room, hands gripping his backpack straps.*)
ALICE. You gonna close the door, dude?
AUGUST. Right. Sorry. (*AUGUST closes the door and returns to the center of the room. ALICE retrieves two*

45

beer bottles from the fridge and approaches AUGUST.)
So...

ALICE. August, right?

AUGUST. Yeah.

ALICE. Cheers. (*Handing him a beer.*) For the nerves.

AUGUST. (*Accepting, questioningly.*) Thank you.

> (*ALICE withdraws a bottle opener and casually pops open her beer. She hands the bottle opener to AUGUST. He stands there dumbfounded. ALICE takes a huge gulp before noticing.*)

ALICE. Bruh.

> (*ALICE snatches the bottle and opener out of AUGUST's hands, snaps open the bottle real quick, then hands AUGUST back the beer.*)

AUGUST. (*Unemphatically.*) ...cheers...

ALICE. Yeah? You ready?

AUGUST. Of course. I've only done it like... a hundred times.

ALICE. Yeah?

AUGUST. ...mostly cans...

ALICE. BOTTOMS UP!

> (*ALICE throws her head back and CHUGS her beer. AUGUST tries but struggles to keep up. She finishes first. ALICE, not letting AUGUST give up, uses her hand to elevate his beer and hold it to his mouth. AUGUST manages to finish without choking, but he struggles to compose himself. ALICE tosses the bottles in the trash and tucks the bottle opener away.*)

AUGUST. Alice, right?

ALICE. My friends call me Allie.

AUGUST. Ok, Allie. My mother's name is Allie.

ALICE. Alice is fine. (*ALICE plops down on the couch.*)

AUGUST. Alice it is.

ALICE. Why the backpack?

AUGUST. Diabetes...

ALICE. Cool.

AUGUST. It's not serious. I just have chocolate bars in

case I need 'em.

ALICE. Gimme.

AUGUST. What?

ALICE. Your chocolate. I'm hungry.

AUGUST. Right, but I need 'em... just in case.

ALICE. In case of what?

AUGUST. In case I need 'em.

ALICE. I can't have *one*?

AUGUST. Well... I might need it.

ALICE. Fine. Whatever.

AUGUST. I mean, I guess you can have *one*.

ALICE. (*Sarcastic.*) If you don't think you'll need it.

AUGUST. This happens a lot so I always bring extra.

ALICE. Dude, would you sit the fuck down.

AUGUST. Yeah, sorry. (*Sits.*) It's just, I have to use the bathroom.

> (*AUGUST sets his backpack down, gets a chocolate bar from the front pocket and hands it to ALICE.*)

ALICE. (*Unabashedly devouring the chocolate bar.*) What for?

AUGUST. What do you mean? I have to use the bathroom.

ALICE. Right, but like number one or number two?

AUGUST. Neither.

ALICE. Neither???

AUGUST. Um, yeah... I have to... you know.

ALICE. ...Oh, ok. So do it.

AUGUST. Well I don't want to do it in front of you and have you smell it.

ALICE. Ok.

AUGUST. Right. So...

ALICE. So just do it.

AUGUST. Right. Ok.

ALICE. Right.

AUGUST. It's just... I just don't feel comfortable. (*A moment.*)

ALICE. Dude, just fucking fart. I've been farting since you came in.

AUGUST. Wait... What?

47

ALICE. Yeah, I've literally been farting this entire time.

AUGUST. What? Um. OK. Yeah. I guess I'll just fart then.

ALICE. Yeah. (*AUGUST shifts his bum, squints a bit, then settles back in. Beat.*) Did you have eggs this morning?

AUGUST. No, did you?

ALICE. Yeah. (*A moment.*)

AUGUST. So are we gonna have sex now?

ALICE. Wait, what?

AUGUST. Isn't that why you invited me over?

ALICE. What? No.

AUGUST. Oh. Sorry.

ALICE. Wait, so you came over here thinking I wanted to have sex with you?

AUGUST. I thought that's why you invited me over.

ALICE. Would you have come otherwise?

AUGUST. Um... I don't know. I just - I thought that's why you invited me over.

ALICE. No.

AUGUST. Oh. Sorry. I'll just leave then.

ALICE. Why would you think that?

AUGUST. Oh. I don't know.

ALICE. You think I'm easy?

AUGUST. Um... No.

ALICE. That I'm a slut? That I just invite guys over to fuck them?

AUGUST. I don't think that would make you a slut. Why wouldn't you invite guys over to fuck them? Women like sex too, right? Anyway, I just figured you liked sex and that's why you invited me over. Unless - unless you've never had sex before. Have you never had sex before? Oh, sorry. I shouldn't've asked that. Sorry. I'll just go then.

ALICE. No, wait... Let's do it!

AUGUST. Seriously?

ALICE. Yeah.

AUGUST. Oh. Ok. Um... Like now?

ALICE. No, next week.

AUGUST. Oh. OK.

ALICE. Yes, now!

AUGUST. Oh. OK. Cool... Like here? Like on the couch?

ALICE. Yeah. Is that OK?

AUGUST. I don't know. Is it gonna be enough room?

ALICE. I don't know. You tell me. You're the expert.

AUGUST. Yeah, I think we'll be OK.

ALICE. Great.

AUGUST. Wait, isn't your dad coming home soon?

ALICE. Not for another hour.

AUGUST. Awesome. That's just enough time.

ALICE. Does it really take that long?

AUGUST. Is that not normal?

ALICE. I don't know. I don't think so.

AUGUST. Right. Well I was just joking anyway.

ALICE. Shouldn't you know?

AUGUST. Yeah. I know. I was just joking.

ALICE. Oh my God. You're like totally a virgin too.

AUGUST. What? No. Yes.

ALICE. Wow. Wow. What a fuck boy. That was so fucked up.

AUGUST. Sorry.

ALICE. And you tried to make me feel bad for being a virgin.

AUGUST. That *was* arguably fucked up and I'm sorry.

ALICE. What do you mean, "arguably?" That was fucked up. You literally tried to make me feel bad for being a virgin.

AUGUST. One could argue that.

ALICE. Whatever. This was a mistake.

> *(ALICE gets up and goes to the door, but before she can open it:)*

AUGUST. (*Wide-eyed.*) You're so pretty.

> *(ALICE is taken aback. For once, she has no quick-witted response. Her irritated, hard exterior melts away. Her cheeks turn a beet RED as she brushes back her hair.)*

ALICE. Really?

AUGUST. Really.

49

ALICE. It's the make-up.

AUGUST. It's not the make-up. It's you. I think you're beautiful without the products.

ALICE. You've never seen me without make-up.

AUGUST. I have. At Charlie's. When you make beer runs for your pops. He's my neighbor. You're beyond perfect just the way you are.

> *(ALICE, hand on the door knob, definitively grips the lock instead, engaging it with a twist. She then makes her way over to the switch, cuts OFF the LIGHTS, and snags a cover to throw over her and AUGUST.)*

> *[NOTE: The following intimacy occurs out-of-view of the audience, under the cover. Thus, besides the kiss, the action can and should be simulated.]*

ALICE. OK. Um... Did you want to take my clothes off? Or should I? I can - I can do it.

AUGUST. Wait, we should kiss first.

ALICE. Right. Sorry.

AUGUST. No, you're fine.

ALICE. Um, like how should we do this?

AUGUST. Oh. I think it's just supposed to happen.

ALICE. Right. Ok. (*They KISS.*) That was good. Was that good?

AUGUST. That was good.

ALICE. Oh my God. Sorry. I'm sorry.

AUGUST. For what?

ALICE. Your - your thing.

AUGUST. Oh wow. Yes. My thing.

ALICE. It's big. Is it big?

AUGUST. I don't know.

ALICE. Well it looks big... Sorry.

AUGUST. It's OK... actually, it is big. Way bigger than usual.

ALICE. Shut up... can I touch it?

AUGUST. I mean, yeah... (*She does.*) OWW!!

ALICE. What?

AUGUST. You can't-- You can't squeeze that part!

ALICE. Are you ok?

AUGUST. It's a very sensitive area. You can't just grab it like that.

ALICE. (*Sarcastically.*) Sorry. I'm an ignorant virgin so I didn't know. (*AUGUST stares at ALICE a moment. He's falling head over heels for her quick wit. ALICE suddenly becomes self-conscious.*) What is it?

AUGUST. Nothing.

> (*AUGUST eases ALICE's concerns by pressing his nose to hers. All is well in the world. ALICE is in WONDERLAND.*)

LIGHTS OUT.

ACT I

Scene 4: Ghosts of the Misbegotten

SETTING: *Robin's home. A few hours have passed.*

AT RISE: *SARAH's deceased body lay in a pool of blood. ROBIN, still in street-wear, is asleep on the steps. Footsteps creak the floor boards above. ALICE, now wearing vintage lounge wear, ENTERS, descending the stairs, taking care to step over ROBIN's sleeping person. Whereas one wouldn't normally take any notice, the otherwise quiet house highlights the CREAKING boards with every step she takes.*

At the bottom, a scene of HORROR greets ALICE. Shocked, her body jumps backward. At the same time, her mouth agape, she catches an instinctive and most unfortunate HOWL, uncertain of what threat still remains. Tripping over her too-quick feet, she hits the hardwood floor with a loud, unmistakable CRACK. Her blood boiling, ALICE army-crawls ever so slowly back toward the stairs. Once there, she nudges ROBIN. No response. Undeterred, she SMACKS him repeatedly, practically beating him. Still, nothing. The floor boards above CREAK again.

LUIS. (O.S.) Alice! Was that you?... Alice, dear, is everything alright!? (*LUIS, still dressed for work, tracks past the staircase on the way to the master bedroom.*) Alice! Where are you?
  (*LUIS tracks back, searching desperately for ALICE. He spies her at the base of the steps.*)
LUIS. (CONT'D) (*Descending.*) ALICE!!! Thank God I

found you. What was that awful smack I heard? And why the devil are you on the floor? That's no place for a lady. (*LUIS, not even acknowledging ROBIN, steps over him and meets ALICE. All the while, she's been signaling for him to be quiet. He took no notice, until now.*) What's the matter, dear?

(*ALICE directs LUIS' attention to the bloody scene. He reacts in great contrast to ALICE: LUIS SHRIEKS out loud in a pitch so high an eight-year-old girl might strain to hit it. LUIS doesn't stop there. He shrieks again and again. His body reacts no better as he hops and high-knee skips about. Carelessly, he lands a hop [or maybe a skip] directly in SARAH's blood, splashing but a corpuscle onto ALICE's hand. She FREAKS. ALICE SPRINGS to her feet in athletic fashion. GALLOPING, she shakes her hand about violently, hoping the drop of blood will magically fly away. It doesn't. LUIS ceases his hopping and skipping to help ALICE. He WRESTLES ALICE to the sink where he rubs clean the drop of blood.*)

LUIS. (CONT'D) Out, damned spot! Out, I say!

ALICE. I think you got it!

LUIS. Best to be sure.

ALICE. I said, you got it!

(*ALICE YANKS her hand free from LUIS. Still high on adrenaline, they look to each other for a moment and then the room. Then, back to each other. Discovering in SYNC:*)

ALICE & LUIS. ROBIN!

ALICE. That lunatic! He's killed someone!

LUIS. He's guilty of something, I'm certain. But not that.

ALICE. You're right. He's too... well, drunk.

LUIS. Right! It couldn't possibly have been him! He's been passed out this whole time. I'd know. That's how he sleeps.

ALICE. I'm calling the police!

LUIS. Good-- Wait, bad! Very bad!

ALICE. What?

LUIS. *We* know Robin's innocent, but *they* won't.

ALICE. Ok, but what about her? She may still be alive. Every second we waste, we could be responsible for her death.

LUIS. Alice... she's dead already. You don't lose that much blood and suddenly come to in the hospital.

ALICE. (*Hyperventilating.*) Oh no. I think I need to sit down.

> (*Breathing in and out audibly, ALICE makes her way to the couch and sits. She pulls her knees tight to her chest and tucks her head between them. LUIS gets a closer look at the deceased.*)

LUIS. (*Recognizing her.*) Alice, do you know who this is? (*No response.*) This is Sarah. Robin's ex-wife... Things just got a whole lot more complicated. (*LUIS goes to the sink and fills up a jug with cold water.*)

ALICE. What are you doing?

LUIS. Sobering up our fool.

ALICE. I really think we should call the police. What if whoever did this is still in the house?

LUIS. I believe they are. Bleeding out on the floor.

ALICE. You think she killed herself? With what?

LUIS. I think, it's highly unlikely someone would break in just to kill an unwanted guest. Then stick around and touch nothing. Look, everything is just as we left it. Everything, except for her.

ALICE. I hope you're right.

LUIS. Hope's overrated. I prefer facts.

> (*LUIS makes his way to ROBIN halfway up the stairs and proceeds to empty the jug of cold water over his head. ROBIN JOLTS awake.*)

ROBIN. What the Hell!? (*ROBIN, jumping off the steps too quickly, SLIPS and falls into SARAH's puddle of BLOOD. He lands face-to-face with the recently deceased.*) AHHHHHHHHHH! (*ROBIN tries his best to stand, but it's slippery. He manages to compose himself, but now he's COVERED in SARAH's*

BLOOD.) Anyone care to explain why my fuck ugly ex-wife is bleeding out in my living room?

LUIS. We were hoping you could do the honors.

ROBIN. Nope. Definitely not. I may have blacked out, but I damn sure would've remembered her hideous mug staining my brand-new hardwood floor.

ALICE. (*Shaking in the fetal position*.) We have to call the police.

ROBIN. NO! They'll arrest me on the spot.

LUIS. Whatever happened to having nothing to do with it?

ROBIN. That ain't how it looks.

ALICE. Well we have to call someone. When my parents died, I called 911 immediately. There was nothing they could do, but maybe it's not too late for her. You may not have killed Sarah, but you'd be just as guilty for not trying to save her.

ROBIN. Sarah is dead, Alice... and since when do you know Sarah?? (*ROBIN looks to LUIS who throws his hands up*.)

ALICE. Are you a doctor now?

ROBIN. All of her blood is *outside* of her body. And like with your parents, you don't have to be a doctor to accept the obvious reality, however unbearable... Sarah being the one who's dead makes this pretty bearable though. Considering.

LUIS. Check her pulse.

ROBIN. You check her pulse.

LUIS. But you're already covered in her blood. No sense in getting my DNA mixed up in the equation too. (*ROBIN checks her pulse*.) Well? Let's hear it.

ROBIN. Just as we feared. She's still utterly fuckin' repulsive. Even in death.

LUIS. (*A light bulb goes off*.) Let's call the Chief. He still owes you a favor as I recall.

ROBIN. Now you're thinking! After performing at his retarded daughter's disaster of a wedding, he owes me big time.

LUIS. It wasn't as bad as you say. It was actually quite sweet. They were a good match, those two.

ROBIN. A model couple. Like Ike and Tina.

ALICE. Just call the Chief already! I'm freaking out, guys. There's a dead woman in the living room. Now I definitely can't stay here.

(LUIS dials on the telecom over the bar. A dial tone RINGS three times until TONY, the Chief of Police, answers.)

TONY. (V.O.) Who is this?

ROBIN. Tony, it's me! Robin.

TONY. (V.O.) Hey! What's goin' on, funny man?

ROBIN. You deleted my number?

TONY. (V.O.) No, no. New phone.

ROBIN. Listen, I got a favor to ask. You got a minute?

TONY. (V.O.) Dealing with a murder-suicide at the moment... but I guess the perp ain't goin' nowhere. Besides, I've been meaning to talk to you.

ROBIN. You're the best, Tony. Just stop by as soon as you can. It's urgent.

TONY. (V.O.) Everything alright?

ROBIN. Not exactly.

TONY. (V.O.) Guess that's why it's urgent, right?

ROBIN. Right.

TONY. (V.O.) I'll be there in five. Luis, you there?

LUIS. Indeed, sir.

TONY. (V.O.) Mind gettin' a pot of coffee goin' for me? The receptionist called off today so we're all chuggin' along at half-speed.

LUIS. Of course, sir.

TONY. (V.O.) Appreciate it. (*TONY hangs up.*)

ROBIN. Boy is he gonna regret having me work his retarded daughter's wedding when he sees this.

LUIS. (*Starting a pot of coffee.*) I think he regretted that immediately. This will be salt in the wound, as you people say.

ROBIN. You've lived here over twenty years. Please stop saying you "people." Nothing but animals on this side of the pond.

ALICE. (*Gesturing toward ROBIN.*) Exhibit 'A.'

ROBIN. Nature vs. Nurture. I'm a product of my surroundings. What does that say about you?

ALICE. That you were never around. Thank God.

LUIS. That's enough! The Chief of fucking Police is on his way. This place *looks* like a crime scene, let alone *is*. We need to clean up. Perhaps then we'll have a chance in Hell at convincing a thirty-year veteran of the force we're not some bumbling crew of half-witted murderers.

ALICE. So long as it's you asking, I'd be happy to help.

> *(With the scent of fresh coffee permeating the room, ALICE and LUIS begin to clean up. ROBIN is of little use as he has no idea where anything goes. ALICE should have a similar issue, but her intuition spares her. ROBIN tries to help.)*

LUIS. Maybe you should just sit this one out. (*LUIS motions to reference ROBIN's hands. They are soaked in blood.*)

ALICE. Not like you were gonna be much help anyway.

> *(Frustrated that he is of little use cleaning, ROBIN goes to move SARAH's body.)*

LUIS. What in God's name are you doing?

ROBIN. When Tony gets here, do you really want the first thing that he sees to be my dead ex-wife?

LUIS. I suppose not, but you're disturbing the crime scene. Tampering with evidence is a crime itself. Best to leave her where she lies.

ROBIN. Lying is her natural state. (*ROBIN shifts SARAH's body back exactly as it was.*)

LUIS. (*Smacking the back of ROBIN's head.*) Enough! This is no time for humor.

ROBIN. Easy. You're this close to being unemployed.

LUIS. Ha! Good luck with that. You put this house in my name six months ago for fear you wouldn't live much longer. Right now, you're a guest in *my* house. May you be so lucky as to remain one.

> *(A car pulls up and SCREECHES to a halt O.S.)*

ALICE. That was fast.

ROBIN. I didn't think she'd be that easy to move either. I remember her being quite the heifer. Must've finally lost weight after bleeding out.

ALICE. No, the Chief. I just heard him pull up.

ROBIN. The donut shop is next door.

LUIS. Almost finished!

(The front double doors SWING open with the kick of the Chief's boot. ENTER TONY, the Chief, in full uniform. The now-dry beer about the entrance lends his shoes an annoying stickiness. TONY stops to take in the scene. ROBIN is covered in blood. SARAH's lifeless body is straddled beneath him. LUIS has a case of flop-sweat as he tries to act normal. ALICE, fairing no better, has the truth written all over her face.)

TONY. Fuck me.

(TONY turns and tries to BOLT, but ROBIN stops him by blocking the door. As ROBIN moves about, blood tracks with him.)

ROBIN. Wait! Please, I promise there's a reasonable explanation.

TONY. Ok, let's hear it.

ROBIN. Really?

TONY. NO! Now step aside. I'm calling it in.

LUIS. (*Stepping in.*) Chief, please. If I may, we're not asking you to compromise yourself. We just ask for some discretion.

TONY. What are you suggesting?

LUIS. It'll be a zoo before you know it if you call it in now. Just get one man, someone you trust. He'll come alone, look her over, tell us if he suspects foul play. If not, then we all get on quietly. No one will think you didn't do your job. You just didn't want to cause alarm and waste anyone's time.

TONY. And if he does?

LUIS. We've no bargaining chips, Chief. We're at your mercy. But for all the many faults of Mr. Summerville, surely you don't think him a murderer?

TONY. If he suspects foul play, then this becomes a high-profile homicide. And some powerful people are gonna be asking a lot of questions. They're gonna wanna know why I didn't immediately devote all available resources. Why I kept it quiet wasting an hour or so of precious time. And yeah, not wanting to cause alarm before I was certain is a good answer, but they're not gonna care. If it was anybody else, they'd say I did the right thing. But they hate Robin. And they've been dying for an excuse to burn him and anyone near him.

(ALICE, who has been hiding her face since the Chief entered, reveals herself and makes a final plea on ROBIN's behalf.)

ALICE. Do it for me.

(TONY is awestruck. He approaches ALICE with great reverence.)

TONY. Miss Alice? I hadn't realized you'd been placed in Robin's care as of yet.

ALICE. They moved the funeral up and Robin got released early to attend.

TONY. Then they wished you luck, huh? Bastards!

ALICE. My uncle Robin is a drunk and a coward. He's a callous jerk and a disappointment to everyone he's ever known. He's even a no-good, piece-of-shit, poor excuse for a father. He's a lot of things, but he's no murderer. I'm sorry if he's hurt you in the past - he's hurt a lot of people - but even the worst among us deserve a second chance. And we'd be no better if we stooped to his level.

TONY. Of course, Miss Alice. I know just who to call. *(TONY makes a private call. LUIS and ROBIN are stunned by ALICE's pull with the Chief. TONY hangs up.)* He'll be here shortly. *(Addressing ROBIN.)* You better be telling the truth.

ROBIN. You two good friends?

TONY. I was the first responder... have you told them?

ALICE. No.

ROBIN. Told us what?

TONY. It's not my business to say.

LUIS. But Chief, with all due respect, Miss Alice is a minor. And Robin is her guardian - for now anyway. If it's serious, he has a right to know.

TONY. It's only because of her that I'm helping him. Don't push it.

ROBIN. Her dad was a piece of shit who murdered her mom and then himself. What more is there?

ALICE. That's it. Congratulations, you know the whole the story.

(TONY gets a call. He reads some missed texts before answering.)

TONY. It's my guy. He's calling back, says it's urgent. (*Answering.*) Yeah, I saw your texts. What's going on?

(TONY is quiet for the rest of the phone call. He hangs up without exchanging any pleasantries for goodbye.)

LUIS. Is there a problem, sir?

TONY. Where's the remote?

(ROBIN fetches the remote and hands it to TONY. He turns on the TV. The loud hum of the speakers makes the anxious group jump. He then navigates to the proper channel. It's the news.)

[NOTE: The TV is not a real prop on stage. The down stage center audience serves as the TV. Therefore, the following news segment need only be audio, and not visual.]

(They listen intently as the reporter, a female, delivers the following:)

REPORTER. (V.O.) Breaking news: Celebrity comedian, Robin Summerville, often described as the "best to ever do it" by his contemporaries before his sudden and very public fall from grace - which featured the comedian violently drunk and obscene on innumerable occasions - now finds himself the subject of a new and developing scandal. I - and I alone - am in possession of a private recording in which the disgraced comic can be heard giving alcohol and other drugs to a minor as well as a provocative picture. The substance of which you won't believe. More at 11!

(ROBIN snatches the remote from TONY and cuts the TV off. The room falls silent. Nobody knows what to think or say. Beat.)

LUIS. (*Chipper.*) Coffee, anyone?

(A moment longer, then:)

LIGHTS OUT.

ACT I

Scene 5: A Deal with the Devil

SETTING: ***Robin's home***. *The weather is delightful as warm sunlight enlivens the space. A great commotion can be heard outside. The occasional flash of light reminds us of the paparazzi's presence.*

AT RISE: *LUIS, professional as always, prepares some coffee. ALICE, in casual designer clothes, is eating a sandwich like an animal. TONY, in full uniform, stands ready for action. LUIS looks to TONY to offer a cup of coffee. He nods in the affirmative and LUIS happily obliges. They exchange pleasantries ("Your coffee, sir," and "Thank you"). The coffee's excellence is practically inscribed on TONY's face.*

ROBIN ENTERS, stumbling clumsily down the stairs. He's putting the finishing touches on a tux: the buttons are misaligned and his shirt is untucked. LUIS swoops in to assist.

ROBIN. How do I look?

ALICE. Like Jesus right before his crucifixion.

ROBIN. That bad, huh?

ALICE. (*Chewing, inaudible.*) No, you look good.

ROBIN. (*Mocking her.*) Naw, jewook gerd. (*Clearly.*) Finish chewing, Alice.

ALICE. Sorry... (*Finishes chewing.*) I said, you look like shit.

ROBIN. Much better.

LUIS. That's enough, you two!

TONY. (*Sipping his coffee.*) She's not wrong.

LUIS. No, she's not. But that's why I'm here. Come, let's fix your hair.

ROBIN. At least we can fix *my* hair.

> *(Re: TONY's bald head. LUIS whisks ROBIN away to the bathroom, leaving ALICE and TONY alone. ALICE finishes her sandwich and proceeds to wash the dishes haphazardly.)*

TONY. What an insufferable idiot! I'm so sorry, Miss Alice, that fate has placed you within his orbit.

ALICE. Fate has also placed me within your orbit. And Luis' orbit. So I can't be too mad.

TONY. Luis is one-of-a-kind. If there were no Robin and Luis was your guardian, I could confidently leave you in his care and my job would be done.

ALICE. It's not your job to make sure I have a good home.

TONY. I made it my job.

ALICE. *(Finishing with the dishes.)* I'm emancipated. I can take care of myself.

TONY. No you're not, Miss Alice. You're no freer now than you were a week ago... I had my detectives double check your petition themselves. Came back to me with 90% confidence it was a forgery. The court is in the process of revoking its decision as we speak.

ALICE. NO! What have you done? I can't stay here with that selfish maniac! He's as toxic as arsenic.

TONY. I'm so sorry, Alice. I really am. I wish there were something I could do, but your documents were falsified. Interestingly though, not by you. By your dad. Mind telling what interest your father had in having you legally declared an adult?

ALICE. *(Mortified.)* I wouldn't know.

TONY. *(Privately.)* Alice, it's ok. You can tell me. I promise, I won't go digging up graves. It'll just be between us.

ALICE. There's nothing to tell, so dig all you want.

TONY. Clever girl. You think you've got everyone fooled, but you can't fool me.

ALICE. What's so special about you?

TONY. I don't overlook the details.

ALICE. You don't know anything! I'm just some kid that

nobody cares about. So stop pretending.

TONY. You're wrong. I care. That's why I took this job. So I could help those that nobody else cared about. When I lost my parents in a fire, I had nobody. Like you. So I know how that feels. I know how it feels when you have nothing else to live for and you're just begging for it to be over. I know how it feels when you shut down because the hurt is too much to bear and you think no one around you can handle your pain, so you just bury it. I know how it feels to pretend that everything is ok even when you're dying inside. Alice, believe me, I know. And that's why I'm here. So you can try to get rid of me all you want, but I'm not going anywhere. You're stuck with me 'til the very end.

ALICE. You're here because there's a mob outside.

TONY. I'm the Chief. I could've assigned anyone I wanted to this detail. But I didn't.

ALICE. Of course not. This is too high profile. And you're under great scrutiny. You said it yourself.

TONY. That's all true, but everything changed when I saw you that night. It was as if I'd seen a ghost... If the circumstances were different and this wasn't a high-profile case and I didn't have my superiors breathing down my neck, I'd still be here. Just for you.

ALICE. I don't believe you.

TONY. Believe this: when I found out you'd be forced to live with Robin, I asked the Judge to consider granting me guardianship instead. Last night, he agreed. On one condition... that you consent all on your own. You've had enough men force your hand. It's time you made your own decisions.

ALICE. Don't flatter yourself. It's not like I have a real choice. I can't stay here.

TONY. Still, we wanted to give you the option.

ALICE. Do you have daughters of your own?

TONY. Yes... I did. Two. And you nearly had a /daughter of your own.

[NOTE: It's better if the audience can't make out the end of TONY's line here ("/daughter of your own") due to ALICE talking over him.]

ALICE. What are their names?

TONY. Were.

ALICE. What *were* their names?

TONY. Meredith... she was our second child. The baby.

ALICE. That the retarded one?

TONY. Yeah... I guess Robin still hasn't lived that one down. Good.

ALICE. He thinks you owe him one for it. He thinks that's why you're here.

TONY. Figures.

ALICE. And the other?

TONY. (*Momentarily entranced.*) That necklace. I haven't seen it in some 16 years.

ALICE. I almost forgot I had it on. It's lovely, but it's just so gaudy... (*ALICE removes the necklace and returns it to the drawer she got it from.*) You've seen it before? Robin said it belonged to his late wife. What was she like? (*TONY can't bring himself to speak.*) It's ok. You don't have to say. How about your first daughter? What's her name?

TONY. Was.

ALICE. What *was* her name?

TONY. ...Alison.

(*ALICE is STUNNED. ROBIN and LUIS ENTER. ROBIN is finally presentable. LUIS is exasperated.*)

ROBIN. (*Oblivious to the tension.*) How do I look?

ALICE. Like Jesus *after* his crucifixion.

LUIS. Miss Alice!

ALICE. Fine... you look good, Robin.

ROBIN. Alice, please, swallow before you speak.

ALICE. I'm not even eating, anymore.

ROBIN. Perfect. Now, what was it you said?

ALICE. I said, you look like shit, Robin.

ROBIN. Well, I did tell Luis to make me look more like

65

you.

> *(RING, RING, RING. The intercom system on the wall flashes red. LUIS goes to the wall and presses a button.)*

LUIS. *(Into the intercom.)* Hello? This is Luis. Master of the house.

AURORA. (V.O.) Hi. This is Aurora. With Channel 7--

LUIS. *(Interrupting.)* My dear Aurora, how do you do?

AURORA. (V.O.) Nervous, and now anxious too. I'm at the address you sent me, but there's a million people here crowding the entrance. Any idea how I might get in?

LUIS. We have the Chief of Police with us. We'll send him out to get you. How might he identify you?

AURORA. (V.O.) Red pumps.

LUIS. ...How *else* might he identify you?

ALICE. *(Interjecting.)* Come around the back. You can scale the tree on the east side up to the balcony with sliding glass doors. No one will see you.

AURORA. (V.O.) Who was that?

LUIS. Miss Alice. The heiress of the manor. She's right, of course, but the climb... it's not for the faint of heart.

AURORA. (V.O.) I'm not some valley girl. Give me a minute, I'll be right up.

TONY. I'll help you.

AURORA. (V.O.) Who was that?

LUIS. That was the Chief of Police. You're in good hands, Miss...

AURORA. (V.O.) Aurora.

ROBIN. Aurora... Borealis??

AURORA. (V.O.) ...Yes. Aurora Borealis.

ROBIN. Really? How did I know that? Have we burned the midnight oil, you and I?

LUIS. Robin! Have you no manners?

AURORA. (V.O.) ...Yes, Robin. We have. *(The room fills with an awkwardness.)*

LUIS. *(Saving face.)* ...Miss Aurora, we look forward to your... ascension. *(Hanging up.)* If you were a rogue train, I don't think you could derail this more than you already have.

ROBIN. So, we've nothing to fear. It's all uphill from here.

ALICE. (*Cringing.*) It's weird when you rhyme accidentally.

ROBIN. Who said it was an accident?

ALICE. My last 24-hours with you. I don't think you're capable of having an intention and following through with it.

TONY. I like her.

LUIS. She's good people.

ROBIN. What's so great about 'teen's choice' over here?

ALICE. Where should I begin?

ROBIN. Why don't you start at the part where I give a damn.

ALICE. Funny. You were begging me to stay yesterday, but now that you have an audience, you all of a sudden want nothing to do with me. Toxic masculinity. Ever heard of it?

ROBIN. Ugh. You did not just say that.

ALICE. You're afraid of being vulnerable in front of other men so you act tough.

ROBIN. I knew what you meant, but why'd you have to use those feminist buzzwords?

ALICE. I didn't know they'd trigger you so much.

ROBIN. Take them back and I'll be vulnerable for a second in front of these big strong men. I pinky swear.

TONY. This ought to be good.

LUIS. We're hanging on your every word, Mr. Summerville.

ALICE. Fine. I take 'em back. Now let's hear it.

(*LUIS hands ROBIN a cup of coffee. ROBIN slips some whiskey in it for a little pick-me-up.*)

ROBIN. For the record, Miss Alice, I do love you. And I do want you to stay. But I want you to want to stay and, as you made quite clear yesterday, you don't. And I'm hurt. After all, I am your father.

ALICE. In name only.

ROBIN. Believe me, I get it. You have no shortage of reasons to leave.

ALICE. And no reasons at all to stay.

ROBIN. And yet, I wish you would.

ALICE. Well, you could've fooled me.

TONY. You certainly fooled me.

LUIS. Robin only repartees with those he loves.

ROBIN. Thank you, Luisa.

LUIS. I pray the reporter buries you, to save me the trouble.

TONY. Speak of the devil.

(AURORA appears on the balcony outside the sliding glass doors. She's holding her red pumps and there's debris in her hair. TONY goes to let her in.)

ROBIN. Yikes. That was morbid.

ALICE. Luis is only morbid with those he loves.

(TONY slides open the glass doors. AURORA, a mid-30s reporter in a none-too revealing, business-formal outfit and glasses, ENTERS in a huff. She passes by TONY and finds her way to the living room.)

TONY. So much for helping you up.

AURORA. It was nothing. *(AURORA struggles to straighten up and clear the debris from her hair and outfit.)*

LUIS. Allow me.

AURORA. I'm all yours. *(LUIS offers his assistance and AURORA gives him all access without a second's thought. ALICE joins to touch up her make-up.)* You both are life savers. Thank you.

ALICE. It's whatever. But in the future, I'd go easy on the make-up. You don't need it.

AURORA. Thanks... I guess.

LUIS. That's her way of saying you're pretty without it.

AURORA. Oh! Well, thank you!

LUIS. No, thank *you*. We appreciate you working with us on this most sensitive of matters.

AURORA. It wasn't easy convincing my boss to let me go in without cameras, but exclusive access to the man of the hour wasn't something they could pass up. (*Turning her attention to ROBIN.*) Speaking of which, you ready, champ?

ROBIN. I was born ready.

AURORA. Dear God, are you drinking already?

ROBIN. Aren't you a breath of fresh air.

AURORA. It's ten in the morning.

ROBIN. Better late than never.

AURORA. Please tell me you've made other arrangements for the kid?

TONY. Already taken care of, ma'am.

ALICE. I'm not a kid.

AURORA. Please don't call me "ma'am." Do I really look that old?

ALICE. I'm telling you, it's the make-up, dude. It ages you.

AURORA. Let's not get frisky so soon. I *just* got here.

ROBIN. Only an hour late. I was surprised to hear you knew the time.

AURORA. I know a lot of things that would surprise you.

ROBIN. And I thought I was the only comedian in the room.

AURORA. I was never going to be a beauty queen or win any popularity contests.

TONY. So instead you made a career out of ruining the lives of people with actual talent.

AURORA. Somebody's gotta do it.

ALICE. That time of the month, huh?

AURORA. I'm a successful woman in the modern era so I'm no stranger to the sexist remarks from the chauvinistic pigs that liter the workforce, but worse than the men are the women. You'd feign to hear some of the awful whisperings I get from short skirts in high heels. Women are vicious.

ALICE. Geez! I was just making a joke, lady.

THE COMEDIAN

TONY. It's my fault. I shouldn't have joined Robin in judging the motivations of our guest. I've no idea why you people do the things you do, Robin included. I just despise the celebrity personality. And you press who glorify them are no better. The example you all set for our youth is despicable. It's a miracle any kids at all turn out as good as Alice. But I digress... Luis, your coffee is too strong. I'm all wound up.

LUIS. Have some of Robin's. He seems pretty loose.

AURORA. I'm here for a quote, not an indictment. You good to get started, sea-legs? (*AURORA prepares a mic and local recording device on her person.*)

ROBIN. Why do you think I'm drinking?

AURORA. (*Starts recording.*) Sarah, your ex-wife, sent me a recording yesterday--

ROBIN. (*Suddenly lively.*) I remember you now.

AURORA. You do? I was beginning to worry you never would.

ROBIN. How could I ever forget? It's not every day a one-night-stand testifies against you in divorce court.

AURORA. I'm glad you're not still bitter.

ROBIN. The night is young.

AURORA. Again, it's ten in the morning.

ROBIN. Well, it's night somewhere.

ALICE. I bet he didn't even know he was cheating on Sarah. You two do share a striking resemblance.

AURORA. We look nothing alike.

TONY. Add beer goggles to the equation and you two could be sisters. It is rather uncanny.

ROBIN. Make it whiskey goggles and you've got twins, easy.

AURORA. He tried that angle in court.

ROBIN. Judge wasn't buying it.

AURORA. It got a few silent laughs.

ALICE. Because it resonated?

AURORA. Because it was preposterous.

ROBIN. Sarah's waist was never quite so slim. Her diet of sucking the fun out of everything kept her nice and fat.

AURORA. I'm blushing. Did Robin Summerville just call me thin?

ROBIN. You should see Sarah now. She's lost a few pounds.

LUIS. Enough! Aurora, please, continue.

TONY. Wait! Isn't this a conflict of interest? She's been with the accused.

AURORA. Oh, we'll get to conflicts of interest. Don't you worry.

ALICE. Been with the accused? Bruh, this ain't court.

LUIS. Please, everyone, let's allow our guest to do her job.

AURORA. (*A moment while AURORA collects herself and starts again.*) As I was saying... Sarah, your ex-wife, sent me a recording yesterday. I knew who she was of course. After all, her lawyers are the ones who convinced me to testify on her behalf. But I'd never spoken to her outside of that so I was confused. Why would she send me a recording? Then I listened to it. And what I heard disgusted me. I immediately ran the story. But as you know, it's illegal to record someone on private property and the recording is inadmissible in court if it was done without the other party knowing and consenting. So, I ran the story with no physical evidence. Just first-person testimony from a confidential source. "Failed comedian has inappropriate relationship with underage girl." Before I could even finish my segment, news breaks that Sarah - the very same Sarah we've been talking about - your ex-wife, was found dead. Here! At your residence! Mere hours after contacting me, my confidential source on a major story winds up dead in the house of the very person she was squealing on. What are the chances of that? Now I'm here for a comment. And we paid top dollar to be the only ones.

ROBIN. Alice, you can thank this wanna-be Sarah right here and the pigs at Channel 7 for sending you to college in a few years.

ALICE. Thank you?

71

AURORA. Sarah's death was ruled an accident.

TONY. Because it was an accident. The only trauma to her body was to the back of her head which she hit when she slipped and fell backward, knocking herself unconscious. The glass from a broken bottle was sharp enough, and the impact hard enough, to penetrate deep resulting in massive blood loss. She would've lived just fine from all of that, but no one was here to help her. So she bled out. I said all this last night at the press conference and the coroner confirmed it.

AURORA. So it's all just a big coincidence then? Come on. I thought cops were supposed to be more inquisitive than that.

TONY. The optics aren't good, but we don't arrest people because of bad optics. We look at the evidence. And the evidence is clear. There was no foul play.

AURORA. That's ridiculous. Ever seen that staircase series on *Netflix*? No way someone bleeds out from a fall like that.

TONY. It wasn't just a fall. There was glass.

AURORA. And that brings us full circle back to conflicts of interest. It's obvious you're covering for Robin because he married your daughter twenty years ago and they had a kid. And there she is right there. And she looks just like her. Doesn't she? She died too though, didn't she? How many women have to die around Robin before you start doing your job? Who's next? Alice?

TONY. I know what you're doing, but it won't work. I'm not gonna be pushed to an emotional outburst and reveal some grand conspiracy. Robin was drunk enough to be in a coma. Even now he can barely string a sentence together.

AURORA. Speaking of whom... got anything to add, Captain Jack-ass?

ROBIN. Thank God that bitch is dead.

LUIS. Robin!

AURORA. I'm glad you think this is funny. Because the

recording wasn't the only thing Sarah sent me.

(AURORA pulls out her cell phone and shows off the picture of ROBIN and ALICE kissing. Gasps all around. TONY launches at ROBIN and punches him square in the face, instantly dropping him.)

LUIS. You can't reveal that picture. It was taken illegally.

AURORA. True. But I didn't obtain it through illegal means. The recording and picture were sent to me, not solicited *by* me. So technically, I can show it.

ALICE. Then why bother paying all that money? Just to shove it in our faces before you ruin our lives?

(ROBIN shakes off the punch. His lip is cut.)

ROBIN. Because... it's a better story. Confronting the bad guy.

LUIS. Miss Aurora, please don't do this. You won't just be destroying Robin's life. There are two people in that picture. An innocent 16-year-old girl.

AURORA. Her face will be blurred. You know that.

LUIS. That will hardly matter. It'll be a national scandal. Miss Alice will never have a chance at a normal life.

AURORA. Robin ruined her chances at a normal life when he abandoned her at the hospital 16 years ago. My job here is done. I've got a story to write.

(AURORA stops the recording and swiftly makes her way back to the sliding glass doors, ready to make her exit.)

ALICE. I kissed *him*.

(AURORA comes to a dead stop, letting her hands off the doors. She turns.)

AURORA. What?

ALICE. I said... I kissed *him*. Print what you want about the drugs and the drinking... that won't shock anyone. But don't make him out to be some incestuous pedophile. That was my dad. Not Robin, but my dad who raised me.

AURORA. Now that's a story.

ALICE. How long you got?

AURORA. My schedule just cleared up. *(ALICE and*

73

THE COMEDIAN

AURORA take a seat on the couch. AURORA starts recording once again.)

ALICE. Let's start from the beginning.

(Just as ALICE forces herself to relive her trauma:)

LIGHTS OUT.

END OF ACT I

ACT II

Scene 1: Alice Through the Looking-Glass

SETTING: *Alice's home. One week ago.*

AT RISE: *ALICE paces back and forth. AUGUST ENTERS carrying his signature backpack.*

ALICE. Hey.

AUGUST. Hey.

ALICE. Did you get it?

AUGUST. Yeah. No sweat. Cashier couldn't hide her judgement/ but I guess it's to be expected. I mean, look at me.

ALICE. Cathleen, that bitch... If you're looking for a pity party, you're fishing in the wrong pond.

AUGUST. You could at least pretend to like... you know...

ALICE. What?

AUGUST. I get it. I'm not in your league. But you picked me so like... you could at least like... you don't gotta be so mean is all.

ALICE. (*Softening.*) ...Sorry.

AUGUST. It's cool. Here.

> (*AUGUST takes out a small grocery bag from his backpack and hands it to ALICE. He sets his backpack down next to the couch.*)

ALICE. What now?

AUGUST. Now you pee on it.

ALICE. No, I mean like... like what do we do if like... we're still kids ourselves.

AUGUST. I don't know.

ALICE. I was thinking maybe I should... you know... Well, what do you think?

AUGUST. We don't even know if you are yet.

ALICE. But if I am?

75

AUGUST. Why are you asking me? You're 'Miss Independent.' You don't need a man. I mean, you talk to me like you're annoyed you even have to deal with me. I'm not stupid. I know I'm not worth your time. But guess what: you're a fucking mess too, so how do you think I feel? You think I enjoy being vulnerable in front of a girl who's embarrassed to be seen with me? Meanwhile, she's a goddamn train-wreck herself? Well - newsflash - I don't.

ALICE. You're kinda hot when you talk back to me.

AUGUST. Really?

ALICE. I said "kinda." And don't ever raise your voice at me again.

AUGUST. Sorry. (*ALICE punches AUGUST in the shoulder*.) Ow! What was that for?

ALICE. I'm scared.

AUGUST. I'm scared too. (*ALICE punches him again.*) OWW! What was *that* for?

ALICE. Stop being so nice to me.

AUGUST. I'm about to.

ALICE. Ok, I think I'm ready. Wish me luck.

AUGUST. Good luck. (*ALICE punches AUGUST one last time. She dashes for the safety of the bathroom before AUGUST has a chance to retaliate*.) Son-of-a-bit--

ALICE. (O.S.) "Good luck?" That was such a stupid thing to say. You deserved it.

AUGUST. It's exactly what you told me to say.

ALICE. (O.S.) That's how I know you didn't mean it.

AUGUST. You better hope it's positive. Or else.

ALICE. (O.S.) Or else, what? You gonna hit me?

AUGUST. ...No.

ALICE. (O.S.) That's what I thought.

(*AUGUST starts to get a bit woozy. He leans on the couch for support. ALICE does her business.*)

AUGUST. You ok in there?

ALICE. (O.S.) Yeah, it just takes a minute.

(*ALICE ENTERS wielding the test as if it were priceless.*)

AUGUST. What's it say?

ALICE. Are you deaf? I just told you it takes a few minutes. (*Shoving it in his face.*) See?

AUGUST. Woah, chill. You just peed on that.

ALICE. Pee is sterile.

AUGUST. Dude, stop.

ALICE. You don't look so good.

AUGUST. Well there's a lot going on.

ALICE. No, I mean you look sick.

AUGUST. I'm fine.

ALICE. It's ready! Oh my God, it's ready!

AUGUST. What's it say?

ALICE. I'm not ready. I'm not ready.

AUGUST. Give it here. I'll read it.

ALICE. But what about the pee?

AUGUST. It's fine. It's sterile.

ALICE. No it's not! I was quoting a movie, dude. *Dodgeball*, hello??

AUGUST. I've seen it.

ALICE. If you can dodge a ball, you can dodge a pregnancy test!

> (*ALICE chucks the test at AUGUST. It STRIKES him dead in his face. He's too tired to flinch.*)

AUGUST. What was that for?

ALICE. So you haven't seen it.

AUGUST. I've seen parts of it.

ALICE. The parts where the movie wasn't playing.

AUGUST. So it's not sterile?

ALICE. Just read the stick, would ya! (*AUGUST retrieves the test, holding it with minimal skin contact as if it were TOXIC. He reads the results, then FAINTS, hitting the floor with a CRACK. He's conscious, but barely.*) Jesus! August, are you ok? Was it really that bad? (*Checking his vitals.*) August?... Shit! (*ALICE thinks quickly on her feet. She goes to AUGUST's backpack and digs around with haste. She finds a CHOCOLATE BAR and force feeds it to him. Feeling better, AUGUST sits up. He keeps eating.*) Guess you really are diabetic.

For a second, I thought you fainted because of the results.

AUGUST. I did. My blood sugar's fine.

ALICE. But you felt better the moment you had some chocolate.

AUGUST. Who wouldn't feel better after having some chocolate?

ALICE. I thought you were going into a coma, you dope.

AUGUST. It's nice to know you care.

ALICE. Gimme that!

AUGUST. No, it's mine! I have diabetes!

ALICE. Not the chocolate! The test!

(ALICE steals back the test and finally reads the results for herself. She plops down on the couch, defeated. AUGUST wipes his lips, gets serious and joins ALICE on the couch.)

AUGUST. Now we know.

ALICE. So what's the plan?

AUGUST. Figure things out together. We're parents now so our lives are not our own. It's late. We'll talk more in the morning.

ALICE. Stay. Please. I don't want to be alone tonight.

AUGUST. I'm not going anywhere.

(AUGUST gets up to grab a cover and cut OFF the LIGHTS. ALICE and him snuggle up under the cover.)

ALICE. We gotta start coming up with names.

AUGUST. Way ahead of you...

(Before AUGUST can give ALICE any examples:)

LIGHTS FADE.

LIGHTS OUT.

ACT II

Scene 2: My Cup Overfloweth

SETTING: *Robin's home.*

AT RISE: *ROBIN sits alone in silence, same tux as before. LUIS, just getting off the phone, ENTERS with tremendous glee.*

LUIS. Great news! You are officially OFF the black list.
ROBIN. That's racist.
LUIS. Oh, stop it!
ROBIN. Hard to believe the whole black list thing is real.
LUIS. It's very real. Very real indeed.
ROBIN. Alice really saved the day, didn't she?
LUIS. Yes, she did. That was quite courageous of her to step forward and take the bullet for you.
ROBIN. Wonder where she gets that from. Certainly not me.
LUIS. Certainly not. Alison, I imagine. I only knew her briefly, but Alice reminds me of her so much so that sometimes I swear she's risen. I've never been the sentimental type, but she's really done a number on me. I dare say she's inspired me. Given me a new lease on life.
ROBIN. She's inspired me too. I think I'm gonna stick around for as long as I can. So I can watch her grow up. Even if from afar.
LUIS. How wonderful. We should celebrate. (*LUIS opens the fridge, withdrawing a bottle of champagne.*)
ROBIN. You sure you can't stay?
LUIS. I've been eyeing this bottle for years now. It'd be a shame to leave without satisfying my curiosity. But it's such a beautiful bottle. I'd hate to disturb it.
ROBIN. Luis, you don't drink.

79

LUIS. To Hell with what I do or don't do. Get the flutes, damn it!

ROBIN. Yes, ma'am! (*ROBIN obliges.*)

LUIS. That's madame, to you!

ROBIN. Without you, I'd have nothing.

LUIS. And without you, I'd have no one.

ROBIN. So once you're gone, I'll have nothing and you'll have--

LUIS. Me... I've spent these twenty-some years running from myself. It's time I stop focusing on *you* and start focusing on who *I* am. Who *I* want to be. What legacy do *I* want to leave behind. I haven't got much time left.

ROBIN. Same here.

LUIS. (*LUIS retrieves a letter from his coat pocket and hands it to ROBIN.*) Here.

ROBIN. What's this?

LUIS. The deed. Like you, I'm not long for this world. I couldn't possibly bear the burden of this estate if you decided to off yourself prematurely. (*A beat.*)

ROBIN. It's back?

LUIS. My fault. I knew the surgeries were dangerous. But I needed to feel like myself at least once in my life. And now I do. And I'm happy. So if it kills me, then so be it. At least I'll die on my own terms.

ROBIN. Like my mother.

LUIS. Now there's a lion.

ROBIN. That's true courage. I get it now. Not like me at all. If I die, it'll be out of weakness. Self-pity. Self-loathing.

LUIS. (*Triggered.*) How rotten of you! To threaten Miss Alice and myself with your life? To lay that at our feet and make us feel responsible for your perishing? How dare you.

ROBIN. A desperate ploy from a desperate man. I'm sorry, Luis. It was wrong of me. I've made so many mistakes... it's become habit to make new ones.

LUIS. I know, Robin. You're a broken man. I won't hold it against you... just don't try to stop me. You want forgiveness? Then, please, let me go. If you fight me on this... I swear I'll never speak to you again.

(ROBIN takes the champagne from LUIS and pops it open, pouring two full glasses.)

ROBIN. ...Cheers. To old friends.

LUIS. To old friends. Cheers.

(ALICE ENTERS lugging her packed suitcases, all ready to go. She's wearing her mother's dress, taking great caution not to damage it.)

ALICE. Drinking again? Why am I not surprised.

LUIS. Miss Alice!

ALICE. Luis? I thought you didn't drink?

LUIS. And I still don't. Here, let me help you. Robin, lend us a hand. (*ROBIN and LUIS help ALICE down with her luggage, bring it all to the front door.*) Oh Alice, my dear, you must be careful! What happened to the clothes I got you?

ALICE. Nothing. They're on the bed. Already folded.

LUIS. I see...

ALICE. They're nice clothes, but-

LUIS. They're just not you.

ALICE. ...You're a good listener.

ROBIN. (*Referencing her dress.*) And that's all you had left of your own clothes?

ALICE. Thanks to you.

LUIS. (*Sensing the tension.*) Seems like an appropriate time for me to pack my things as well.

(LUIS EXITS upstairs, giving ROBIN and ALICE a moment alone.)

ALICE. He's trying to get us to talk.

ROBIN. I know. He's not as clever as he wants us to think. He shipped most of his stuff last week apparently, so he's only got one bag left to pack.

ALICE. I saw.

ROBIN. So...

ALICE. So...

ROBIN. You're moving in with Tony, huh?

ALICE. For now.

81

ROBIN. Hell of a way to introduce you to your grandfather, right?

ALICE. Right.

ROBIN. He didn't know. That you were still alive. No one knew. Except for Luis.

ALICE. I gathered as much.

ROBIN. Sorry we couldn't make things work here.

ALICE. We could have. I just don't want to.

ROBIN. I know. I was being facetious.

ALICE. You have no idea what that word means.

ROBIN. Not a clue. (*They share a brief laugh.*)

ALICE. Well... I guess this is goodbye.

ROBIN. Forever.

ALICE. (*Confused.*) For now.

ROBIN. Goodbye.

ALICE. Goodbye. (*They stand awkwardly, staring at each other.*) Luis is my ride so I kinda have to wait for him.

ROBIN. Right, right.

> (*Suddenly inspired, ALICE makes her way to the piano. She is drawn to it by some otherworldly force.*)

ALICE. It sucks you don't know how to play. Once I'm gone, this old thing will go back to collecting dust just as it was before.

ROBIN. You want it? It's yours! I'll have it shipped to you.

ALICE. Really?

ROBIN. Of course. Like you said, it's just collecting dust. Better you have it than me.

ALICE. I don't know what to say. First the necklace... now this.

ROBIN. The necklace! Thank you for reminding me. I almost forgot. It's in the dresser, right? Why don't you put it on.

ALICE. I shouldn't. It belongs here. With you.

ROBIN. Nonsense. It belongs with her family. It was their tradition--

ALICE. To pass it down... to the eldest daughter...

(ALICE gets the necklace, puts it on and sits down at the piano. She begins to play the song from earlier but stops as LUIS ENTERS carrying his luggage. It's one bag.)

LUIS. Oh no! Am I interrupting?

ALICE. No. We were just--

ROBIN. We were just--

LUIS. (*Seeing the necklace.*) Feeling nostalgic again.

ROBIN. Exactly.

LUIS. We can't thank you enough, Miss Alice.

ALICE. What for?

LUIS. Reminding us of the things we've lost. And how lucky we were to have had them at all. Robin is not mature enough to say it himself, so I'm saying it for the both of us.

ALICE. This was her dress, wasn't it?

LUIS. Perfectly preserved as if frozen in time.

(ROBIN reaches into his jacket pocket and withdraws a folded-up polaroid. He holds it up so ALICE can see, then tucks it safely in her luggage.)

ALICE. Strange that my mother kept it, *after all these years*.

LUIS. Actually, if I think about it, it isn't strange at all.

ROBIN. (*To himself.*) It's a little strange.

LUIS. So you two got a chance to talk, I presume?

ROBIN. Yeah. We said our goodbyes.

LUIS. Good. Then I guess this is it.

ROBIN. Yeah. I guess so. But let's finish this champagne. After all, you've been dreaming about it for years.

LUIS. That's ok. It was a bit dry for me.

ROBIN. Suit yourself. (*ROBIN gulps down both his and LUIS' glass.*)

LUIS. You enjoy yourself. Alice, take your time. I'll be in the car. Goodbye, Robin.

ROBIN. Goodbye, Luis. Don't be a stranger.

LUIS. No promises. Take care now.

(LUIS EXITS, carrying his bag and most of ALICE's luggage. He leaves behind only one of her bags.)

ROBIN. You should get going, Alice. I don't want to hold you up.

ALICE. You know that song I've been working on?

ROBIN. The melody you were just playing? Yeah. Sorta.

ALICE. I think I just figured it out!

> *(ALICE plays her song. It is the same as before but this time she has exchanged the SOMBER notes for HOPEFUL ones. After playing her song, ALICE stands and makes her way to the door, grabbing her only remaining bag.)*

ROBIN. I'm sorry you lost your baby. (*ALICE stops dead. She is rattled to her very core.*) Guess having a girl ain't so lucky after all.

ALICE. Come on, Robin. I made that up. She needed a good enough story to leave you alone. So I gave her one.

ROBIN. I figured... but I made a few phone calls just to be sure. You were three months along... that what set him off?

> *(Beat.)*

ALICE. ...Yeah.

> *(Beat.)*

ROBIN. ...Was it his?

> *(Beat.)*

ALICE. Goodbye, Robin.

> *(ALICE EXITS, leaving ROBIN behind. All alone, the bad thoughts start creeping in. ROBIN opens his liquor cabinet as the lights fade.)*

LIGHTS OUT.

ACT II

Scene 3: Alice in the Golden Afternoon

REPRISE

SETTING: *Alice's home.*

AT RISE: *ADAM returns to the couch, joining ALICE.*

ADAM. I liked him.

ALICE. No you didn't.

ADAM. You brought him over just to make me jealous.
>   (ADAM puts his hand on ALICE's lap. ALICE
> endures the advance a moment longer than last
> time, before repositioning his hand to the couch
> cushion. ADAM's grip on the cushion intensifies as
> if he were in need of an outlet for his aggression.
> While clutching the furniture, he discovers
> something wedged between the cushions: A
> PREGNANCY TEST. A SHOCK comes over ALICE.
> ADAM is MORTIFIED.)

ALICE. Dad, I can explain--

ADAM. It's positive.

ALICE. Please don't be upset--

ADAM. You're pregnant.

ALICE. I was only hiding it because--

ADAM. You and the kid?

ALICE. ...No.

ADAM. You sure?

ALICE. I'm sure.

ADAM. How far along?

ALICE. Three months. August and I... that was one month
ago.

ADAM. Clever girl. You fooled us both. How d'you do it?

ALICE. Been cutting my wrist for the blood. Short ways,

85

so I didn't bleed out.

ADAM. I raised a warrior.

ALICE. You raised a woman. And now we'll be raising one of our own.

ADAM. We? Isn't that what the kid's for? Poor guy. He's no idea what you're capable of.

ALICE. I did that for us. Our baby needs a father that isn't you or she'll be taken from us. Like I was.

ADAM. You weren't taken from nobody. Your birth mother died in labor. A friend of Robin's with no known family. He knew we were having trouble conceiving so he set up the adoption in secret. He gave you to us. A gift we could never repay. And what a beautiful woman you grew to be. Beautiful as a rose... yet cunning as a spider. And now you've got us men caught up in your web.

ALICE. You act as if I planned this. Daddy... If I'm a spider, it's because I'm helpless. And if it pleased any man to do so, he could squish me without rhyme or reason. I do these awful things because if I didn't, I'd be nothing but a victim. One of these annoying bitches online always crying and demanding sympathy. Going on and on about what she deserves and how hard she's had it. Fuck that. I'd rather bleed in silence than bruise in bellows.

ADAM. You've got a future as a poet. Robin can help you with that. Guy's a mess, but he's got a way with words. And he's all you'll have left so take care of him.

ALICE. What are you talking about?

(ADAM stands, confident. He walks toward the bedroom where EVE is sleeping, leaving his near-empty whiskey on the couch.)

ADAM. *(Stopping momentarily.)* August is a complete fucking idiot, but his father isn't. I've worked with him at the CNC factory a few times over the years. He'll ask for a DNA test and the gig'll be up... I can't let that happen.

(ADAM EXITS to the bedroom, unholstering his

pistol. ALICE tries a different tactic: she races to the landline and dials 911.)

ALICE. (*On the phone*.) Send help! Please!... Send whoever! Just - just please - just send someone!... 87 Elm Drive. Hurry! It's my dad, he's -- yeah that house. That's the one! Exactly, exactly! The same as before!

(BANG. The shock of gunfire knocks the phone right out of ALICE's hand. She slumps down, crying helplessly. ADAM ENTERS, carrying the lifeless body of EVE. Her head is soaked in blood. He sets her down behind the couch and walks over to ALICE. Once there, he hangs up the phone, then walks back to EVE.)

ADAM. I found the pregnancy test. Believing it was Eve's, I went into a blind rage. I killed her-- Baby, you listening? (*ALICE nods through the tears*.) In a blind rage, I killed her. Unable to cope with what I had just done, I carried her out here, hoping to get to the car. To fix what I had done. I'm not strong enough. I set her down. Not ready to give up, I try to resuscitate her. Chest compressions and mouth-to-mouth. I still love her. After no response, mouth-to-mouth turns to a kiss. Our final kiss. My last chance to say goodbye. (*ADAM kisses EVE tenderly*.) Goodbye... forever. (*He reaches over the couch and grabs the whiskey. ADAM turns it upside down, taking huge GULPS*.) Your mother was a saint, but she would've done anything to protect you. Including lie. Then she would've been just as corrupt as me and Hell would be her resting place. But I've sent her to Heaven, so you'll have some company when you go. (*ADAM fights the burn of the whiskey*.) At gun point, I force you to call 911. You oblige. You say exactly what I tell you to say - word for word. I howl in pain. You drop the phone and the line goes flat. You don't know what happened next. (*Red and blue flashing lights puncture the windows and paint the walls*.) You close your eyes... and everything goes dark. (*ALICE forces her eyes closed*.) You try to block it out as best you can. It's too much for a little girl to take... This was the only way, baby. You'll go live with your uncle, far away from the kid, where he can't find you. No one ever has to know the truth. (*A cacophony of sounds creep in. Sirens, heavy footsteps, and men shouting orders.*) Clever girl. You had it all planned out. It was almost perfect. But you overlooked one thing. A father's love knows no bounds... I love you, kiddo.

(*A hard KNOCK. Three times. Then a voice shouts:*)

POLICEMAN. (O.S.) POLICE! OPEN THE DOOR OR WE'LL BREAK IT DOWN!

ADAM. It's a 'she,' huh? What's her name?

ALICE. ...Charlotte.

ADAM. Charlotte... that was her middle name.

(*Resolute, ADAM downs the last of the whiskey like bad medicine and puts the gun to his temple... BANG. Simultaneously, before the carnage can be witnessed: The LIGHTS go OUT. The door is broken in and police secure the room. TIME SKIPS FORWARD a bit.*)

(*LIGHTS UP. A spotlight illuminates only ALICE and the policeman who is revealed to be TONY. There's commotion in the background but it's in darkness. ALICE, wheezing heavily, takes a puff from her inhaler.*)

TONY. It's ok. You don't have to speak much. I'll take your statement later. For now, I just want to know if you have any family who could take you in? (*Getting a clear view of ALICE's face, he stands back in awe as if he's seen a ghost.*) Alison?... (*Suddenly, ALICE keels over in immense PAIN. She CRIES out. Whatever it is, it's unbearable.*) Miss?! You ok?... Medic. MEDIC! I need a medic! (*Brushing ALICE's inner thigh in the chaos, some blood is transferred to TONY's hand. Shocked and confused, he doesn't want to imagine why she would be bleeding from down there.*) She's bleeding!

(Officers and medics crowd ALICE just as:)

LIGHTS OUT.

CURTAIN

ACT II

Scene 2.5: Forever is Goodbye

[NOTE: This scene, should you choose to stage it, shall appear at the end of Act II, Scene 2, as a continuation of the scene. The lights will go down for a few beats, then come back up to indicate the passage of time.]

SETTING: *Robin's home.*

AT RISE: *ROBIN, still wearing the same tux, is in a DRUNKEN haze. He's over the moon. To complement his mood, he throws a vinyl on the record player atop the sticky bar. Getting comfortable, he slings his jacket with intention as if there were a coat rack in its trajectory, but there isn't. It glides gracefully to the floor. The music is transcendental. ROBIN sings and dances along (for as long as desired), drinking more and more all the while.*

[NOTE: This beat could be very long or very short. In any case, it should EPITOMIZE the moment. A calm before the storm. Jubilation before condemnation. "Go all out and leave nothing in the tank," is the general takeaway.]

ROBIN briefly exits then returns with a bottle of red wine. It's a special occasion. He uncorks it and drinks directly from the bottle. He drinks so clumsily that red wine flows down his chin and onto his white shirt, staining it beyond repair. The red is so thick, one could be forgiven for thinking ROBIN SLIT his own THROAT.

Still passionately singing along, ROBIN erects a ladder beneath the beam with a tattered rope. He ascends with a new rope, capable of sustaining his weight. At the top, he throws it over the beam and fashions it around his neck. Before taking the final PLUNGE, he takes the remaining sips from his wine. As he finishes the last of the bottle, ROBIN is stopped dead by a miraculous sight: his dead ex-wife SARAH APPEARS before him. He drops the bottle of wine to the floor. The rope CLINGS to his neck all the while.

ROBIN. (*Struggling to speak.*) Speak of the devil...

SARAH. Not quite.

ROBIN. You've gotta be shitin' me.

SARAH. Don't look so happy to see me. I'll blush.

ROBIN. Lord knows you could use the color.

SARAH. Don't need it. It's all black and white on this side.

ROBIN. How so?

SARAH. There are no races or ethnicities. All you see is someone's soul. The outside doesn't matter. It's what's inside that counts.

ROBIN. What if you're empty inside? What then?

SARAH. No one is truly empty. Even the worst among us have substance, albeit small. But if you're patient, you will see.

ROBIN. So... to what do I owe the pleasure?

SARAH. Your drunken stupor.

ROBIN. Who you callin' "stupid?"

SARAH. Not "stupid," "stupor."

ROBIN. You say tomato, I say tomato. (*ROBIN says "tomato" the same way both times.*)

SARAH. (*Confused, profusely.*) What?

ROBIN. Am I dead?

SARAH. Not yet. But you're about to be.

ROBIN. Don't threaten me with a good time.

SARAH. I'm not.

ROBIN. ...Do you hate me?

SARAH. What do you think?

ROBIN. I think... I think you hate me.

SARAH. I did. Now, I'm not sure. I want to, but I can't.

ROBIN. I hate me too.

SARAH. Look, I came here to raise Hell and make you regret ever meeting me--

ROBIN. Already do--

SARAH. But you're so damn pitiful, I can't even do that.

ROBIN. I'm a piece of shit. No need to bring me down. I'm as down as it gets.

SARAH. Fuck me! I can't believe I'm about to say this, but... you're not a piece of shit.

ROBIN. What was that?

SARAH. I said, you're not a piece of shit.

ROBIN. Sorry, come again?

SARAH. You heard me.

ROBIN. No, seriously. I'm like-- I've got like white noise in my ear.

SARAH. You're not a good man, Robin. But you're not nothing. And you mean so much to that little girl. She needs you. Even if she doesn't know it. She puts on such a good face, but she's barely holding it together. Her soul is in desperate need of mending. You are the only thing standing between her and an early grave. You owe it to her to keep fighting the good fight. She has so much to offer this world.

(A moment while the deepest parts of ROBIN bubble to the surface. His minimal movements thus far have been enough to tug on and tighten the rope around his neck. The more he moves, the less he can.)

ROBIN. I'm drowning and I've no idea how to swim.
(EVE APPEARS.)

EVE. That's no excuse. You fight by never giving up, no matter what. Many great men have had to tread water all the way to shore, never learning how to swim.

ROBIN. Eve? Is that you?

EVE. Yes, it's me.

ROBIN. I never got to thank you... for raising my little girl...

EVE. And you'll never have to. That's what big sisters are for. Helping you when you can't help yourself.

ROBIN. Could've done without the abusive pedophile.

EVE. Were I still living and had I known, I'd be beating myself up for it right now. But it wouldn't make Alice any better off. Having a self-loathing mother.

ROBIN. Instead, she's got a self-loathing father.

EVE. And she's suffering for it. Don't you think she's suffered enough?

ROBIN. You're dead... and Sarah's dead...

EVE. But you're not dead. Not yet.

ROBIN. I know, but... is Alison there?... Can I see her?
    (A beat.)

EVE. You're not done on Earth. You need to stay and make amends. Then you can join us. And you and Alison can spend eternity with one another.

ROBIN. Really? You promise? (*EVE DISAPPEARS.*) Eve? Eve?

SARAH. She's gone. For good this time.

ROBIN. (*Elated, for the first time.*) Did you hear what she said? When I'm done here on Earth, I get to spend eternity with Alison. What a gift.

SARAH. She's lying, Robin.

ROBIN. What? No she's not!

SARAH. Alison isn't down here where we are. (*Fixing her gaze above.*) She's up there. Amongst the stars.

ROBIN. (*Desperate.*) How do I get up there?

SARAH. You can't. You'll be stuck down here with us when you go.

ROBIN. Please... Is there anything I can do to change that?

SARAH. No.

ROBIN. I don't get it. Eve was a saint. Why would she be down here with you?

SARAH. Adultery, it seems.

ROBIN. That's not fair! Her husband was a monster.

SARAH. Life's not fair. (*Beat.*)

ROBIN. You should be happy... bringing me bad news.

SARAH. I should be. You deserve it. But I'm not.

ROBIN. How come?

SARAH. I don't know. I guess it's like they say: some things you just can't take with you. Hate must be one of them.

ROBIN. I thought they were talking about money.

SARAH. Me too... (*SARAH turns to leave, but is stopped by:*)

ROBIN. You were good to me.

SARAH. Excuse me?

ROBIN. It was me. I was the problem. Not you. You were patient and kind. I was bitter and resentful. Still am. There was nothing you could do.

SARAH. But what I did do wasn't any good.

ROBIN. I made you out to be a revengeful bitch. And then, to spite me, you became one.

SARAH. While I find it flattering, don't waste your confessions on the dead. Focus on the living. They may forgive you yet.

ROBIN. I don't want them to. I deserve this rot.

> (*SARAH stays a beat longer, then DISAPPEARS and, as if breaking from a trance, ROBIN COLLAPSES, surrendering to the rope about his neck. To demonstrate the rope's commitment, ROBIN's dead weight swings back and forth [minimally, but enough to hear the creaking of the strained rope and beam]. The sight is unbearable. A man has HANGED himself. For real.*)

> [*NOTE: END SCENE HERE for a true TRAGEDY, otherwise, continue.*]

> (*Before long, ROBIN soils himself. A yellow liquid pools and drains out the bottom of ROBIN's slacks along the seam. Suddenly, ALICE BURSTS through the front doors, still in her mother's dress. Although deeply [and understandably] disturbed, ALICE does not hesitate to rescue ROBIN. ALICE wrestles her*)

94

arms around ROBIN's dangling body and hoists him up just enough to take the pressure off his neck for a moment while she gameplans. The rope is too tight for her to work his head clean of it with ease. She ascends the ladder, still bearing his weight. The task is impossible given her meek stature, but ALICE is determined to see it through. To make matters worse, she begins to WHEEZE. Her inhaler is at TONY's, so she'll have to tough it out.)

(Eventually, ALICE gets high enough to partially rest ROBIN's body on a ladder rung while she works the rope off with a free hand. The dance is delicate and measured, but finally ROBIN is FREED. He drops to the floor like a boulder with a great BANG. Now unobstructed by ROBIN's body, STAINS can clearly be seen on ALICE's dress. She pays them no mind. ALICE's wheezing worsens. She's fighting for every breath. But time is of the essence. ALICE drags ROBIN to the shower. The shower cuts on as she cleans him. Her WHEEZING peaks. She could faint and drown in the shower.)

(The LIGHTS go OUT, her fate unknown... then, the squeeze of an inhaler is HEARD, followed by a deep wheezing inhale. SUDDENLY, after some time, the LIGHTS come back UP. It's the following morning and ALICE is cooking breakfast. She's changed into designer lounge wear. The Sun is shining as bright as ever and the glass doors to the balcony are open, letting in a slight breeze with the crisp morning air.)

(ROBIN EMERGES from the shower in clean clothes, a victim to the bright lights and unbelievably loud ruckus in his head. HUNG OVER, he can barely compose himself. Just another embarrassment to add to the list. ROBIN finds ALICE preparing breakfast in the kitchen. He is DUMBSTRUCK. Humbled beyond belief, he struggles not to cry.)

ROBIN. Thank you.

95

ALICE. You're welcome... DAD.

ROBIN. I wanted to tell you for so long, but-

ALICE. It's alright.

ROBIN. (*Weeping uncontrollably.*) I don't deserve you.

ALICE. Maybe not, but I'm not going anywhere so you better get used to it.

ROBIN. Sorry about your dress. You must hate me.

ALICE. I'm just glad you're ok. Besides, "the stains add character."

ROBIN. ...Nice callback, but those are urine stains. The only character they add is 'homeless.'

ALICE. Perfect. Then we'll be matching. (*ROBIN nearly chokes, laughing so hard.*)

ROBIN. (*Gathering himself.*) You moving back?

ALICE. Dude. No. Look around you. I'm absolutely still gonna live with Tony. No offense, but he's a bit more put together than you.

ROBIN. None taken.

ALICE. But I won't be far. You need me and... I don't know. It feels good to be needed.

ROBIN. Thank you.

ALICE. And... I just want to say... I'm sorry.

(*Beat.*)

ROBIN. What?

ALICE. I'm sorry, Robin.

ROBIN. What? What are saying? Why are you saying sorry? I should be saying sorry. I'm the fuck up. I'm the one who's fucked up everything for you. I should be saying sorry, not you! How dare you! Why would you say that! I've ruined everything! Me! I'm the reason your parents are dead! That was me! I'm the reason you were raped! I did that! I killed your baby! Me! Not you, me!

(*ROBIN continues... falling apart as he does.*)

ALICE. I am sorry, Robin. I'm sorry that you lost your love. I'm sorry that you were hurting so bad, you sabotaged your whole future and gave me up. And I'm sorry that you're still hurting. Your pain must've been unimaginable. You must've felt so alone... And I'm sorry that this entire time, I've been blaming you for everything bad in my life. I'm sorry because, it's not your fault. And blaming you won't make it go away. And I'm sorry most of all that you haven't forgiven yourself, even *after all these years.* You torture yourself more than anybody. That's why I'm saying I'm sorry. Because I forgive you.

(BEAT.)

ROBIN. ...Alison Charlotte. That was her name. You look just like her. With you here, it's like she never left.

ALICE. I get that now. (*ALICE withdraws a polaroid from her pocket, unfolds it and slides it to ROBIN. It's the one he tucked in her luggage previously.*) What was she like?

ROBIN. A ray of uncompromising light in this vast Hell we find ourselves in. She could make all your pains disappear with but a smile.

ALICE. I could really use that right about now.

ROBIN. You and me both...

ALICE. You saved me, you know.

ROBIN. I did?

ALICE. Yeah. I was having an asthma attack after threading your fat ass neck out of that noose. Thought I was gonna die right then and there. But as I was prying your clothes off to get you cleaned, I found this in your coat pocket. (*ALICE holds out an INHALER.*)

ROBIN. No kidding. I got that after your first night here. Your symptoms seemed pretty serious, so I wanted a backup just in case.

ALICE. You care more than you let on. I didn't think you were paying any attention. (*Beat.*)

ROBIN. ...Did you dress me?

ALICE. Yes, but you still need a tie. You've got a meeting at two, and I'll be damned if I let my first client make a fool of me.

ROBIN. What?

ALICE. You're a free agent who nobody wants and I'm in

need of a job. Contract's on the bar. I charge fifty an hour. What's it gonna be?

ROBIN. (*A chuckle, shaking his head.*) Uh-uh. You get paid when I get paid. Twenty percent. Deal?

ALICE. Deal. I just have one rule.

ROBIN. There's always strings attached.

ALICE. Easy.

ROBIN. Lay it on me. (*A beat.*)

ALICE. No more drinking.

ROBIN. ...Ok.

ALICE. Think you can handle that?

ROBIN. No... but for you, I'll try.

(*Beat. A RING at the door.*)

ALICE. Who could that be? Seriously? Everyone we know either has a key, knows they don't need one, is dead, or wants nothing to do with you.

ROBIN. Maybe they're not here for me.

(*ALICE is struck by ROBIN's comment. Who could be here for ALICE? RING. The doorbell is struck again.*)

ALICE. Coming! (*ALICE quickly checks her appearance on a reflective surface. She freshens up her look with little touches here and there, then spritzes an extra dash of perfume for good measure. RING, RING, RING, RING! The doorbell rings incessantly.*) I SAID, I'M COMING!

(*ALICE answers the door. She stands back in AWE. AUGUST ENTERS, wearing his iconic backpack.*)

AUGUST. Hey.

ALICE. (*Practically paralyzed.*) Hey.

AUGUST. Sorry it took me so long to--

(*ALICE interrupts AUGUST's apology with an intense EMBRACE. After some time:*)

ALICE. I'm not pregnant.

AUGUST. I know.

ALICE. The stress...

AUGUST. It's ok.

ALICE. Please don't hate me. I've been nothing but awful to you. I lied to you... I used you...

AUGUST. Alice, I wouldn't wish what you've been through on my worst enemy.

ALICE. August, I'm so glad you're here. But I can't let you stay. I can barely stand to look at you. I'm so embarrassed and ashamed. What you must think of me. I don't deserve you.

AUGUST. Maybe not, but I'm not going anywhere so you better get used to it.

(*BEAT.*)
(*BEAT.*)

ALICE. (*Chocked up.*) How did you know where to find me?

AUGUST. I didn't... *He* did.

(*AUGUST looks to ROBIN. ALICE does the same. ROBIN stands. Despite his inebriated state, he fights to stand with perfect posture, head held high.*)
(*BEAT.*)
(*ALICE, without haste, finds her way to ROBIN. She folds her arms around him as if to never let go. A moment passes before he reciprocates, folding his arms gently around her.*)
(*BEAT.*)

ALICE. How did you know I'd come back?

ROBIN. I didn't... *He* did.

(*ROBIN looks to AUGUST for reference. ALICE does too, looking over her shoulder without breaking from ROBIN.*)
(*BEAT.*)

LIGHTS SLOWLY FADE.

LIGHTS OUT.

END OF SCENE 2.5/ START OF SCENE 3

Please consider leaving a review on Amazon and visit www.scriptdoctoratl.com for more info and to join the Wrender Studios newsletter.

For licensing, please email us at
wrenderstudiosllc@gmail.com

ABOUT THE AUTHOR

Gordon Hinchen's journey into the world of theater began during his high school years at "The Academy for the Performing Arts" in Chagrin Falls, Ohio, where he delved into the craft of acting and stagecraft. His pursuit of further education led him to SUNY Purchase, where he honed his skills in Playwriting/Screenwriting; however, his academic journey didn't end there. Gordon graduated from Cleveland State University (CSU) with a Bachelor of Arts in Mathematics, accompanied by a minor in Theatre Studies, showcasing his diverse interests and talents.

During his time in Cleveland, Gordon made significant contributions to the local theater scene. He led the improv troupe Rare Form Improv (formerly known as Torque Improv) for five years, showcasing his improvisational skills and comedic timing. Simultaneously, he graced the stage in equity productions at Dobama Theatre in Cleveland Heights, delivering memorable performances such as the regional premiere of Annie Baker's Pulitzer

Prize-winning play "The Flick," where he portrayed the main character, Avery. His dedication and talent were recognized when he achieved the prestigious status of becoming a full-fledged member of the esteemed stage actor's union, AEA.

In 2020, Gordon embarked on a new chapter in Atlanta, Georgia, settling in the suburb of Peachtree City to pursue a career in film. With thousands of on-set hours logged as a Production Assistant and Grip, Gordon gained invaluable experience behind the scenes. Now fully immersed in the world of theater and film, Gordon is committed to his craft as a playwright, screenwriter, and script doctor.

When he's not crafting compelling stories, Gordon enjoys quality time with his beloved tri-colored corgi and his supportive wife and best friend, Kelsey. Together, they share a love for classic cinema, culinary adventures, and leisurely strolls around the picturesque lake near their home.

Connect with Gordon Hinchen on Instagram to stay updated on his latest projects and future endeavors.
Instagram: www.instagram.com/gordonhinchen/